A LITTLE LIFE

A LITTLE LIFE

based on the novel by
Hanya Yanagihara

conceived and directed by
Ivo van Hove

adapted by
Koen Tachelet, Ivo van Hove
and Hanya Yanagihara

NICK HERN BOOKS
London
www.nickhernbooks.co.uk

A Nick Hern Book

This adaptation of *A Little Life* first published in Great Britain as a paperback original in 2023 by Nick Hern Books Limited, The Glasshouse, 49a Goldhawk Road, London W12 8QP

A Little Life (novel) copyright © 2015 Hanya Yanagihara, published in the UK by Picador, an imprint of Pan Macmillan

A Little Life (play) copyright © 2023 Koen Tachelet, Ivo van Hove and Hanya Yanagihara

Hanya Yanagihara has asserted her right to be identified as the author of the novel. Koen Tachelet, Ivo van Hove and Hanya Yanagihara have asserted their right to be identified as the authors of this adaptation

Cover: *A Little Life*, TM Davy, 2023 (Oil and canvas, 104h x 68w inches, 264.16h x 172.72w cm). Courtesy of the artist and Company Gallery, New York. From an original photograph by Charlie Gray

Designed and typeset by Nick Hern Books, London
Printed in the UK by Ashford Colour Press, Gosport, Hampshire

A CIP catalogue record for this book is available from the British Library

ISBN 978 1 83094 230 0

CAUTION All rights whatsoever in this play are strictly reserved. Requests to reproduce the text in whole or in part should be addressed to the publisher.

Performing Rights Applications for performance by amateurs or professionals in any medium and in any language throughout the world should be addressed in the first instance to Creative Artists Agency, 405 Lexington Avenue, 19th Floor, New York, NY 10174, USA, *fax* +1 212 277 9099, *email* ross.weiner@caa.com

No performance of any kind may be given unless a licence has been obtained. Applications should be made before rehearsals begin. Publication of this play does not necessarily indicate its availability for amateur performance.

Author's Note
Hanya Yanagihara

A lucky writer gets published. A very lucky writer gets read. An extremely lucky author gets to see her work become beloved. And a profoundly lucky writer gets to witness one of her readers make her creation into something else—a chimera, something she both recognizes and doesn't.

Watching the process of one's book becoming a play means experiencing Roland Barthes' 1967 essay 'The Death of the Author' in real time: Remember, Barthes argues, that 'a text's unity lies not in its origins'—that is, its creator—but in its audience. The author's intentions mean nothing, and she must accept that her illusion of ownership is just that; she must understand that her book, once written, no longer belongs to her—its life and meaning are both bestowed and determined by the reader. This shift in perspective isn't an easy one to make, even when faced with the good fortune of an adaptation. But it's worth it for the complicated, often awe-inspiring sensation of having the chance to see one's work through another's vision.

Writing is a solitary occupation; it depends on no one but the writer. But a play is the original collaborative art form, and as I sat in this play's South London rehearsal space over a week in January and again in February, I marvelled at the number of people who'd assembled to make the work breathe, to make it operate as a single organism: The actors and the director, of course, but also the set and sound and lighting crews, the costume and prop managers, the script supervisors and music technicians. I watched the actors find their way into their characters, an almost physical wrestling akin to one animal burrowing into the skin of another, eventually leaving behind— as they must—their fear of misinterpreting the people I'd written in favour of imagining someone new: a being part mine, part theirs.

The play, as Ivo and his collaborator Koen Tachelet have conceived it, might be seen as a constellation of overlapping and intersecting love affairs—between Jude and Willem, Jude and JB, Jude and Malcolm, Jude and Harold, even Jude and Brother Luke—and I watched too as the actors (I think reflexively) tried to find ways to create intimacy with one another, touching and hugging and in general seeking out any opportunity to make physical contact. The room therefore became the site of dozens of romances, no less real for being conjured so quickly, and in service of work. But the play is also a ghost story, sometimes literally, in the form of the people from Jude's past who haunt his present, and sometimes metaphorically, in the form of the life he might have had—if he hadn't been unlucky. If he hadn't been abandoned. If he'd learned earlier how to talk about his life. I had always thought the book an exploration of how a person makes an accommodation with life; Ivo's play suggests that a human must fight to engage with it, even when (perhaps especially when) that life is at its most impossible. What I think we'd agree on is that the only thing that makes a difficult life bearable is love— the ability to give it, and the ability to receive it as well.

As the author of *A Little Life*, the book, I can't tell you, my fellow audience members, all the reactions you'll have to *A Little Life*, the play. However, I *can* promise you'll be astonished by it. The inventiveness of the stagecraft, the dedication and generosity and vulnerability of the performances, the adaptation's kineticism and velocity—all combine to make a singular theatrical work, one that, love or hate it (and it's not worth making art at all if the only thing you want is for everyone to like it), you won't easily forget. It's a play that changed my life, in ways both anticipated and not: May it change yours as well.

Co-adaptor and Director's Note
Ivo van Hove

Hanya Yanagihara told me that you can read *A Little Life* like a fairy tale about 'a motherless child who has to face horrible challenges and find his own way'. A surprising point of view, considering *A Little Life* is a never-ending, meandering journey through the horrific consequences of the structural, violent sexual abuse of an underage child. *A Little Life* is set in an abstract contemporary time, without any reference to big events like the AIDS epidemic and 9/11. It is completely focused on the emotional life of the characters. *A Little Life* is not a book, it is an excess, an excess of words, feelings, sexual abuse, self-mutilation and heroic attempts at love and friendship. A necessary and stiflingly urgent book. It's a dissection of the social pressure to be happy and successful, of the overvaluation of sexuality in relationships.

It destabilises your entire moral way of thinking. It digs deep into what makes people beautiful, but also into what makes them monsters, to themselves and others. 'A fairy tale', but in the way they were originally intended: to exorcise our dark powers. And one about our world in which the author doesn't give us a solution, no release. A book that is so personal and yet so universal at the same time, rare like a perfect diamond.

The stage adaptation of *A Little Life*—based on the novel by Hanya Yanagihara, and adapted by Koen Tachlet, Ivo van Hove and Hanya Yanagihara—was first performed in Dutch by Toneelgroep Amsterdam (now Internationaal Theater Amsterdam) on 23 September 2018. The production transferred to the Festival Theatre, Edinburgh, as part of the Edinburgh International Festival, on 20 August 2022, and to Brooklyn Academy of Music, New York City, on 20 October 2022.

The first English-language production of the adaptation opened at Richmond Theatre on 14 March 2023, before transferring to the Harold Pinter Theatre, London, on 30 March, and then the Savoy Theatre, London, on 3 July. The cast, creative and production teams were as follows:

CAST
JUDE	James Norton
WILLEM	Luke Thompson
JB	Omari Douglas
MALCOLM	Zach Wyatt
BROTHER LUKE / DR TRAYLOR / CALEB	Elliot Cowan
HAROLD	Zubin Varla
ANA	Nathalie Armin
ANDY	Emilio Doorgasingh

UNDERSTUDIES
MALCOLM / JB	Samson Ajewole
HAROLD / BROTHER LUKE / DR TRAYLOR / CALEB / ANDY	Mark Hammersley
JUDE / WILLEM	Tom Kelsey
ANA	Lorna Lowe

MUSICIANS
Music Supervisor / Cello	Alison Holford
First Violin	Eleanor Parry-Dickinson
Violin	Hazel Correa
Viola	Alison D'Souza

CREATIVE TEAM

Director	Ivo van Hove
Set, Lighting & Video Designer	Jan Versweyveld
Costume Designer	An D'Huys
Music & Sound Designer	Eric Sleichim
Casting	Julia Horan CDG
Hair, Make Up & Prosthetics Designer	Susanna Peretz
Associate Director	Jeff James
Associate Set Designer	Alistair Turner
Associate Lighting Designer	Simon Sherriff
Associate Sound Designer	Rob Bettle for Sound Quiet Time
Associate Video Designer	Mogzi
Intimacy Director & Movement Coach	Sara Green
Fight Director	Bret Yount
Voice Coach	Salvatore Sorce
Costume Supervisor	Poppy Hall
Props Supervisors	Chris Marcus & Jonathan Hall for Marcus Hall Props
Assistant Director	Alice Wordsworth
Assistant Set Designer	Hugo Aguirre
Sound Design Consultant	Erwin Sterk
Associate Set Designer (Original ITA Production)	Bart Van Merode

PRODUCTION TEAM

Production Manager	Lloyd Thomas
Company Stage Manager	Tamsin Withers
Deputy Stage Manager	Natalie Braid
Assistant Stage Managers	Kayleigh Atkinson & Louise Charity
Head of Sound	Elliot Williams
Deputy Head of Sound	Nick Mann
Head of Wardrobe	Jordan Colls
Deputy Head of Wardrobe	Shevonne Harper
Head of Hair, Makeup & Prosthetics	Caz Walters
Wardrobe, Hair, Makeup & Prosthetics Assistant	Jules Green

Head of Automation & Special Effects	Rohan Carr
Lighting & Video Operator	Jake Ayris
Tech Swing	Nathan Boulton
Marketing Manager	Sam Prudhoe-Zdzieblo for Playful Productions
Advertising & Marketing	AKA
Ticketing & Sales	Nat McCormack
Press & PR	Kate Morley
Rehearsal & Production Photographer	Jan Versweyveld
Artwork	Feast Creative
Logo Design	Plastic Palmtree & Adrian Salpeter
Onstage paintings by	Eniwaye Oluwaseyi
Production Mental Health & Wellbeing Support	Applause for Thought & Victoria Abbott

PRODUCERS

Producer & General Manager	Wessex Grove
Producers	Gavin Kalin Productions
	Nia Janis for Playful Productions
Co-Producers	Creative Partners Productions
	Eilene Davidson Productions
	Patrick Gracey Productions
	ROYO
	Rupert Gavin & Mallory Factor Partnership
	New Frame Productions / David Adkin
	Roth-Manella Productions
Originally produced by	Internationaal Theater Amsterdam

A LITTLE LIFE

based on the novel by
Hanya Yanagihara

conceived and directed by
Ivo van Hove

adapted by
Koen Tachelet, Ivo van Hove and Hanya Yanagihara

Characters

JUDE
WILLEM
JB
MALCOLM
ANDY
HAROLD
BROTHER LUKE
ANA
CALEB
DR TRAYLOR

Part I

1.

We're in a small TriBeCa apartment. The four friends gather on the floor; there's a box of mostly eaten pizza nearby. WILLEM, JB, *and* MALCOLM *are smoking blunts. The three raise their beers to* JB.

WILLEM. Happy birthday, JB.

JB. Jesus. If this is how my thirtieth year begins, I don't have a good feeling about it.

MALCOLM. What do you mean?

JB. What do you mean, what do I mean? How'd I end up spending my special day—

MALCOLM. Your 'special day,' oh my god.

JB. —my *special day* helping Jude and Willem move into their latest shitty apartment?

WILLEM. I don't think it's *that* bad.

JB. Willem. *Of course* it's that bad. You two're just inured to how bad it is because it's marginally better than your *last* shitty apartment. And by marginally better, I mean there are mice instead of rats.

MALCOLM. *You* lived with your mom until a month ago, JB.

JB. I wouldn't start in with me about living at home, Mal. (*To* JUDE.) I don't understand why you didn't just stay at Mal's parents'.

JUDE. I couldn't have stayed at Malcolm's parents' forever—they'd have killed me at some point.

MALCOLM. You? Never. Me? Maybe.

JB. But there's only one bedroom! What's next, one bed?

MALCOLM. You know, I was thinking: You guys could build a Sheetrock wall right over there and carve out another space.

WILLEM. Oh, good idea.

JB. And I suppose I'm going to be made to assist in this construction project.

JUDE. It's not *so* bad, JB. Anyway, there's an elevator here.

JB. See, this is what I mean—the fact that the existence of an elevator feels like some sort of major life victory means you suffer from chronic low expectations. And guess what: The elevator doesn't even seem to work! Speaking of which—let's do it.

MALCOLM. Do what?

JB. 'Do what.' Take stock of our lives, of course.

MALCOLM. Oh god, JB. Shouldn't you just be taking stock of *your* life?

JB. No, of course not. It's our tradition. We need to record, among witnesses, where we are in our lives on our birthdays.

MALCOLM. Do we really, though?

JB. I'll go first. JB Marion, thirty, Black, athletic build—

WILLEM. Uhh...

JB. Fuck you, Willem. *Athletic build*. Currently of Nolita...

MALCOLM. ...where you're mooching off of...

JB. ...where I'm providing *intellectual stimulation and artistic services* in exchange for housing. Fairly certain to be one of the most important figurative painters of his generation as soon as anyone bothers to recognize that fact. Tenant of—

MALCOLM. *Sub*-tenant.

JB. *Tenant* of a new shared studio space in Long Island City. Willem, you go next.

WILLEM. Wait, that's it? I feel some key facts are being left out of this self-portrait.

JB. Willem! Go!

WILLEM. JB! I'm not doing this!

JB. Fine, I'll do it for you. Willem Ragnarsson: Also thirty. White as walls. Still has a good head of hair, though who knows for how long. Allegedly good-looking, according to white heteronormative standards. Serial womanizer. Actor.

WILLEM. Waiter.

JB. *Actor*.

WILLEM. Well, thanks, JB.

JB. Talented. But completely without ambition.

Malcolm Irvine. Wasting *his* considerable and real talents by working as a cog in one of the most pretentious architecture firms in the city: Ratstar, named for an Edna St Vincent Millay poem—

MALCOLM. It's actually an Anne Sexton poem—

JB. —instead of doing what he should do, which is striking out on his own. But is so afraid of disappointing his parents, including his father, the Black investment bank CEO—

MALCOLM. —he's actually the chairman, not the CEO—

JB. —by leaving said prestigious firm that he instead just stays put, making useless maquettes—

MALCOLM. It's clear you have no idea what an architect actually does all day—

JB. —while wasting the final shreds of his youth. *Also* completely without ambition. The only Black man I know in New York who's claimed to never have had an issue hailing a cab. The only Black man I know who pretends to live on Lexington because he's too embarrassed to admit he lives *in a house* off Park. With, as noted, his parents.

MALCOLM (*to* WILLEM). Wait, *why* are we still friends with him again?

JB. And then there's Jude.

Jude St Francis.

WILLEM. Okay, JB, let's call it a night. Don't we have to get to that party, anyway? Mal, where is it?

MALCOLM. Let me check. Close, though. Somewhere on Centre Street...

JB. Jude St Francis. Seems to have been twenty-eight for a *very* long time now. Apparently brilliant, though what do I know? Assistant prosecutor at the US Attorney General's office. Ambitious, but to what end? Seems determined not to make money by spending his life in public service. Have no idea what he does all day, but I *do* know that whatever it is, all he can afford is a one-bedroom apartment in Chinatown on an obscure street that he shares with his college roommate.

MALCOLM. *Our* college roommate. Also, technically, this is TriBeCa.

JB. Jude St Francis. Origins: Unknown. Sexuality: Unknown. Past: Unknown. Post-sexual, post-historical. The Postman. Jude the Postman.

JUDE. Thank you for that succinct assessment, JB.

WILLEM. Yes, thanks, JB. Helpful as always. God, you're obnoxious when you're high.

JB. Actually, Judy, I want to ask you a question.

JUDE. I'm not sure I want to hear this.

JB. Well. We've all known each other for a while now…

WILLEM. Wait. *We have?*

JB. Shut up, Willem. And we want to know why you've never told us what happened to your legs.

WILLEM. Oh, JB. That's not true.

MALCOLM. Yeah, Jude. It really hurts our feelings. Don't you trust us?

WILLEM. 'It really hurts our feelings.' Come on, Mal. Don't be a dick. I hate it when you do this.

MALCOLM. Do what?

WILLEM. Use someone else to deflect the attention from yourself.

MALCOLM. I don't do that!

WILLEM. And why exactly is this information relevant at right this moment?

JB. Willem! Stop trying to change the subject! We're talking about Jude now.

WILLEM. This is so stupid.

JUDE. Well. It's just not very interesting.

JB. That's for us to decide.

JUDE. It was the year before I met you guys. I was fifteen. It was a car injury.

JB. Oh. That sucks. I'm sorry, Jude.

MALCOLM. So you—you didn't have problems walking before?

JUDE. No. (*Pause.*) I could even run cross-country.

MALCOLM. Oh, wow.

JB. Man. That really sucks.

WILLEM. A car 'injury'?

JUDE. It was a car accident.

WILLEM. But you said an 'injury.'

JUDE. I meant an accident.

2.

MALCOLM. C'mon, guys, it's almost midnight—we said we'd be there by now.

They leave, JUDE *in the middle,* MALCOLM *and* WILLEM *on either side of him, close enough to catch him should he slip, but not close enough so that* JUDE *would notice they're anticipating his fall.*

At the party, JB *hovers outside the group, focused and taking pictures.*

JB. Normally at parties I bound from one group to the next, gathering gossip, starting rumors, getting drunk. But tonight, I don't drink anything, I don't smoke anything.

I travel around them, my friends, taking pictures of them. The only one who notices is Jude, who watches me—I see him doing it, even though he's trying to hide it. He's always watching—but I'm watching him back.

Sometimes I feel I'm not a part of them. There they are, they're happy without me. It's as if all I have to do is step away from them and suddenly, I don't belong anymore.

What they don't understand is how much I see—or rather, they *do* understand, but they think it's a joke; they think I'm always making fun of them. But that's not true—or at least, it's not only true. They don't get that I see what they can't.

I've been following them for the past few months. I tell them that I'm gathering images for color studies, but I'm actually painting them. My friends. Their lives. Every moment that they don't even realize they're living. I take a picture of Willem waiting to audition, studying his script, one foot pressed against the sticky red wall behind him. I take a picture of Malcolm on a sofa a few feet away from his father, the two of them watching a Buñuel film but never looking at each other. I take a picture of Willem smiling at some girl, a picture of Malcolm running after a cab, like someone's chasing him.

WILLEM. Jude, are you okay?

JUDE. Yes, yes, I'm fine.

WILLEM. Are you sure?

JUDE. Yes, I'm fine. I'm just going to sit down for a minute.

WILLEM. Wait, I'll come sit with you.

JUDE. No—no, Willem, don't. I'm going to be fine. Stay with Malcolm and JB.

WILLEM. But—

JB *is still taking photographs.*

JB. And then there's Jude. I take a picture of him watching a play, his face half-lit, the second he smiles (I nearly get thrown out of the theater for that). Any artist will tell you that the subject they like most, that they treasure the most, is the one who doesn't want to be a subject at all. But I know he won't make me stop, because he—because he loves me. Because he wants me to succeed. I take a picture of him with Harold, Harold smiling at him, Jude smiling at the onions he's chopping. I take a picture of him trying to walk downstairs to the Canal Street station without holding the railing.

But I'm keeping a secret from him. I have a painting I made of him, based on a photo he didn't see me take. He was sitting on the edge of his bed, his forehead against the wall, his arms and legs crossed; he was coming out of one of his episodes with his back. It's a great painting: The colors, the expression on his face, his utter unselfconsciousness because he didn't know I was watching him. But he'll hate it—he'll think he looks too fragile, too vulnerable. And he'll find other things to hate about it, too, things I can't even anticipate.

He won't want me to show it. But I know I will. It's all I have in me. It's mine.

The party rages on.

3.

It's night. WILLEM *is asleep.* JUDE *wakes him.*

JUDE. Willem. Willem.

WILLEM. Jude. What's wrong? What happened to your arm?

JUDE. I'm sorry.

WILLEM. What's wrong?

JUDE. I had—an accident. Will you take me to Andy's?

WILLEM. What kind of accident?

JUDE. I cut myself. We need a cab.

WILLEM. What happened?

JUDE. We need a cab.

WILLEM. Jude—you look terrible; you're shaking.

JUDE. Don't, Willem—please.

At ANDY*'s.*

ANDY. I'm going to unwrap the towel now, Jude.

There's blood everywhere. On JUDE*'s T-shirt, on the floor, the walls. On* ANDY*'s sweater.*

Fuck, Jude.

JUDE. I'm sorry, Andy.

ANDY *finishes tending to the wound.*

ANDY. Willem: I need to talk to you. Now. Did you know he was cutting himself like this?

WILLEM. No.

ANDY. Is he eating regularly, sleeping? Does he seem out of sorts? Has he been depressed?

WILLEM. Jesus, Andy, I don't know. He's seemed the same as always.

ANDY. Well, you *are* living with him, Willem. So I'm telling you now, plainly: If he starts behaving strangely at all, call me immediately. And make sure he eats something when he wakes up.

WILLEM. *I don't know; I didn't know*. That's how all conversations about Jude end. Malcolm, JB, me, even Andy. Even now, we still respect the unspoken agreement we have with him: no demands, no shouting, no threats. So we don't talk about it—not with Jude and not with one another, and we hope the questions we don't ask will just…disappear.

But I'm tired, I'm so tired.

JUDE. Willem. Malcolm and JB are coming over. I'm not going to have time to bake anything.

WILLEM. Jesus Christ, Jude. Fuck your baking.

(*Angry*.) Tell me, what were you actually doing?

JUDE. What do you mean?

WILLEM. You *know* what I mean.

JUDE. Willem—it's not what you think. I promise you. I'm fine.

Do you believe me?

Part II

1.

HAROLD. First he was my student, one of the most brilliant I ever had. Then he became my child. I'm not one of those people who feels that the love for a child is a superior love, more meaningful and grander than any other. But it *is* a singular love, because its foundation is fear. Every day, your first thought is not 'I love him,' but 'How is he?' It's a magnificent kind of love, because the fear behind it is also magnificent.

That was one thing I learned. Here's another: it doesn't matter how old that child is, or how he became yours. Once you decide to think of him as your child, something changes. Everything you have previously enjoyed about and felt for them is preceded first by that fear, that fear that stems from the impossible desire to triumph over the things that want to destroy what's yours.

And here's another: When your child dies, you feel everything that everyone says you will: everything that's been so well-documented, in poetry and song. But here's what no one says: a part of you, a very tiny part of you, also feels relief. Because the moment you've been fearing, preparing for, has finally come. *Ah*, you tell yourself; *it's arrived. Here it is.* And after that, you have nothing to fear again.

JUDE *hums 'Ich bin der Welt abhanden gekomen'*.

Nice. Mahler?

JUDE. Yes. Sullivan asked me to sing it for him yesterday at my interview.

HAROLD. Of course he did.

JUDE. It hardly seems like the most effective way for a federal judge to screen potential law clerks.

HAROLD. That's Sullivan for you. He asks me for students with political views other than his own. The more extreme, the better.

JUDE. So you sent me?

HAROLD. Of course I sent you.

JUDE. Well, he knows opera. He asked me to sing him something that revealed something of who I was.

HAROLD. So you sang Mahler.

JUDE. Yes, and I'm not really sure why — I don't really *like* Mahler. Or this lieder, for that matter: It's too slow, too mournful, too subtle.

(*He sings.*)
Ich bin der Welt abhanden gekommen,
Mit der ich sonst viele Zeit verdorben,
Es ist mir gar nichts daran gelegen,
Ob sie mich für gestorben hält,
Ich kann auch gar nichts sagen dagegen,
Denn wirklich bin ich gestorben der Welt.

HAROLD. 'Ich bin der Welt abhanden gekommen'. I am lost to the world.

JUDE. I was always taught it was about losing oneself *from* the world, about disappearing into a different place, one of retreat and safety. But not as an escape — more as a discovery.

JUDE *continues singing Mahler.*

HAROLD. Who taught you how to sing like that?

JUDE. The brothers.

2.

JUDE. Father Gabriel said I was found inside a garbage can stuffed with discarded food: eggshells, slimy lettuce, spoiled spaghetti.

BROTHER LUKE. Jude, you mustn't believe everything Father Gabriel says. The truth is you were found *next* to the garbage can, in an alley behind a drugstore. But you were lucky you were found when you were: it was April; it was freezing; there was snow on the ground.

JUDE. There were tracks, right, Brother Luke?

BROTHER LUKE. Yes, footprints that led to the bin, and then away from it.

JUDE. Sneakers, a woman's size eight.

BROTHER LUKE. I don't know, Jude.

JUDE. Did they ever look for the woman?

BROTHER LUKE. I don't know, Jude. I'm sure they did.

JUDE. Why wasn't I adopted?

BROTHER LUKE. They tried—but the state couldn't find anyone. This is a poor town, Jude, in a poor county.

JUDE. Something must've been wrong with me for no one to want me. Maybe I cried so much that my mother just couldn't stand it any longer.

BROTHER LUKE. You came here. You're here now. The monastery is your home. There's no point in thinking about the past, Jude.

A change of scene. HAROLD, *holding a suit.*

HAROLD. I have something for you.

JUDE. I have work to do, Harold.

HAROLD. It's *for* your work. I got you something you'll need. Two suits: A dark gray, a navy blue. A dozen shirts.

JUDE. Harold...

HAROLD. Some sweaters, ties, socks and shoes. You can't start working for Sullivan wearing what you're wearing.

JUDE. Harold—I can't accept this. (*Pause.*) Anyway, you taught me never to accept anything.

HAROLD. In the courtroom, that's true. But not in life. In life, Jude, sometimes nice things happen to good people. They don't happen that often. But when they do, it's up to the good people to just say 'thank you,' and move on.

JUDE. But how am I ever going to repay you?

HAROLD. There is no repaying me. This is the end of this discussion.

JUDE gets dressed in front of the mirror.

A change of scene.

JUDE. I am five. Brother Peter's tortoiseshell comb had disappeared. *You little thief!* It had fallen behind a radiator. But soon after that I start stealing for real. A packet of crackers. A button. I know I'm going to be blamed anyway, so I steal more and more. Things I see, shiny things, mostly. One day I steal Father Gabriel's silver lighter—I hide it in my underwear. But when I bump into Father Gabriel, the lighter falls onto the floor. He takes me away; I'm going to be punished. He pours olive oil onto his handkerchief, he rubs the oil on the back of my left hand, he takes his lighter, he holds my hand under the flame, the oil catches fire, my hand is swallowed by a ghostly glow... (*He screams.*) Father Gabriel hits me in the face: *Stop screaming. Now you'll never steal again.*

BROTHER LUKE. Jude — do you want to help me take care of the daffodils?

A change of scene.

HAROLD. But Jude — you're right that law isn't life, and once you begin studying the law, the world begins to look very different. You learn to see not just the problem in front of you, but the rat's tail of problems that might follow it. A house becomes not just a shelter, but a contract, a lien, a site of future lawsuits, of possible violations. There comes a time when students realize that the law is inescapable in daily life, after which life becomes temporarily unbearable. But if you think like this all the time, you'd go crazy.

The biggest thing students struggle with, though, is the difference between the law and justice; or, more simply and profoundly, the difference between law and fairness. There's always a student who says 'but that isn't fair.' But not you.

JUDE. No, I don't find fairness that interesting.

HAROLD. Fascinating. Someone young who doesn't believe in fairness.

JUDE. Fairness is for happy people — for people who grew up with certainty.

But for scared people, life isn't about fairness — it's about what's right.

Pause.

HAROLD. I'm not sure I agree. (*Pause.*) But Jude — you look really nice in that suit.

JUDE. Everything covered, everything hidden. Now I can be anyone. Someone blank and invisible.

HAROLD. Tell me, Jude, where did you grow up?

JUDE. Montana and South Dakota, mostly.

HAROLD. So are your parents ranchers?

JUDE. It's beautiful countryside out there. Have you spent any time there?

HAROLD. That's the silkiest pivot I've heard in a long time. Do you see them often?

JUDE. They're dead.

HAROLD. I'm sorry, Jude. (*Pause*.) So are mine. But then, I'm much older than you. Were you close?

JUDE. Not really.

HAROLD. But I'll bet they were proud of you. (*Pause*.) Are you in a relationship?

JUDE (*angry*). You're really interested in this.

HAROLD. I'm not interested in *this*, but in *you*. What's strange about that? This is the kind of stuff friends talk about.

JUDE. Then maybe we can't be friends, Harold.

A change of scene.

JUDE. After my hand heals, I'm summoned back to Father Gabriel's. *Take off your clothes.*

A change of scene.

BROTHER LUKE. You don't deserve what happens to you, Jude. I would never hurt you, you know that, don't you?

HAROLD. I understand you don't want to talk about it. So what shall we talk about instead?

JUDE. How about—how about...math?

HAROLD. Math.

JUDE. Yes. Pure math.

HAROLD. What's the difference?

JUDE. Regular math, or applied math, is used to provide solutions—in economics, or engineering, or accounting. Pure math, though, doesn't exist to provide immediate, or necessarily obvious, practical applications. It's purely an expression of form, if you will—the only thing it proves is the almost infinite elasticity of mathematics itself (within the accepted set of assumptions by which we define it, of course). A beautiful proof is succinct, like a beautiful ruling. It combines just a handful of different concepts, albeit from across the mathematical universe, and leads to a grand and new generalized truth: that is, a wholly provable, unshakable absolute in a constructed world with very few unshakable absolutes.

HAROLD. Absolute certainty. In a constructed world.

JUDE. At times I imagine that Harold is my father, someone I trust completely—but only if he accepts that the first fifteen years of my life must remain unspoken.

BROTHER LUKE. If you were with me, I'd never hurt you. We'd have such a wonderful time. We could go camping together. I'd teach you how to fish. We'd live in a little cabin, like a father and son. We'd grow all our vegetables in our garden, and flowers, too. You want to grow pumpkins, right?

JUDE. Yes—yes, I want that.

ANA. Was that the moment?

JUDE (*silence*).

ANA. The moment when you later knew: *this is when it happened, this is where it started.*

JUDE (*silence*).

ANA. The moment you gave up everything to follow Brother Luke.

JUDE. That was the moment.

ANA. I can teach you.

JUDE. What?

ANA. To talk about it. About what happened all those years, all those years ago. What it did to you.

JUDE. Ana, I don't see why. You know who I am. You read my file. *You're* my social worker. I don't want to *talk* about those years—I want to forget them. Can you teach me that?

ANA. Maybe you'll find your own way to talk about it. You'll have to, if you ever…

JUDE. If I ever what?

ANA. Want to be close to anyone.

JUDE. Then maybe I never will.

ANA. Jude—no matter what you think, you have nothing to be ashamed of, and none of it has been your fault. Will you remember that?

JUDE. You shouldn't have done this to me, Ana. You convinced me to stay alive and then you die. You left me alone, without anyone who knows me.

3.

JUDE *comes home from work. His hands are shaking. He can't manage to get the key in the lock. He curses and drops his keys, then picks them up and manages to open the door.*

JUDE. Another fifteen steps to the bed.

Fourteen...

Thirteen...

I'm going to have to call Andy. I'm going to have to call him again.

I'm so selfish. I should have been in a wheelchair a long time ago. But I can't, and now I'm having to reach out for help to people who have been helping me for years.

Ana...

ANA. I'm here. Hold my hand.

JUDE. It doesn't help.

ANA. Do it anyway. And count to a hundred. You know this, Jude: it divides the pain into portions. Count until it stops.

JUDE. One, two...

JUDE *lets* ANDY *undress him and lays down on the table.* ANDY *removes the bandage from* JUDE*'s leg and pulls the soaked gauze underneath from the raw skin.*

ANDY. Jude — your refusal to listen to me about anything that concerns your body is either a pathological case of self-destructiveness or it's a huge fuck-you to the rest of us.

JUDE. Are you going to lecture me?

ANDY. No. I'm getting you a wheelchair.

JUDE. My life — my life — my life.

4.

Preview opening of JB*'s show 'The Boys.'* JB, MALCOLM, WILLEM *and* JUDE *walk past the paintings.*

MALCOLM. JB. These are genius.

WILLEM. They really are, JB.

MALCOLM. But JB, I always knew you were talented. We all did, right? I mean, you're an asshole, but no one ever said you weren't talented. Or that under all that self-absorption there wasn't something real and deep inside.

And now here we are, the boys on the wall.

JB. I recommend you look at everything in one continuous movement. Malcolm—no. Start over there. There's a *progression* to these images, people: You have to start from the beginning.

JUDE. What's that?

MALCOLM. What?

JUDE. That painting.

MALCOLM. I don't know, but it's great.

JUDE. It's me.

WILLEM. Jude, are you okay?

JUDE (*almost to himself*). JB never showed it to me.

That position I'm in—

MALCOLM. *Jude, After Sickness.*

JUDE. JB, what is this?

JB. Oh, that? That's the best piece in the show.

JUDE. You made a promise to me, JB — you took a picture of me and didn't tell me. I didn't know I was being photographed. You knew and you did it anyway.

JB. You're making a really big deal about this, Jude. It's not like anyone knows who you are.

JUDE. Why can't you just say you're sorry?

MALCOLM. Jude, you know he won't apologize. This is JB. You're wasting your time.

WILLEM. This is fucked up, JB: You told him you'd let him see any picture of himself in advance.

JB. Well, there's nothing I can do about it now!

WILLEM. You could start by taking the painting out of the show and giving it to Jude.

JB. I can't do that! MoMA wants to buy it!

MALCOLM. MoMA!

WILLEM. So what? (*To* JB.) If you're as fucking good as you keep telling us you are, you'll have another shot at MoMA.

JB. That's not the way it works, Willem. Jude, this is your problem, not mine. You're so fucking insecure. It's about time you deal with that.

JUDE. *That's* your answer? That it's *my* fault you lied to me?

JB. What do you want me to do, Jude? Do you want me to destroy it? Should I set it on fire? Would that make you happy? It can't be un-seen, so why can't you just accept it and get over it?

JUDE. I'm not asking you to destroy it, JB — I'm asking you to apologize.

JB. But why should I?

JUDE *walks away.*

He's just walking out of here!

WILLEM. And you don't understand why?

JB. He's not listening!

MALCOLM. What about the painting?

WILLEM. Well, you have to take it down, JB.

JB (*to* WILLEM). You're a traitor. You're *always* taking Jude's side. You know that, right?

WILLEM. If you want to stay Jude's friend—

JB. You don't give a shit about my career. I've always supported yours—*always*.

WILLEM. —and if you want to stay mine, then you'd better, JB.

5.

WILLEM. Malcolm finally leaves Ratstar and opens his own firm.

MALCOLM. Yup: Bellcast. And we have our first public commission—a photography museum in Antwerp.

JUDE. Willem gets his first big film role. He breaks up with his girlfriend.

WILLEM. Jude sees plays with Malcolm.

JUDE. And gallery shows with Willem.

MALCOLM. A whole list of things we would have once done together that we now do instead in twos or threes.

JUDE. I miss JB.

WILLEM. I know. I do, too.

JUDE. But I just can't forgive him. I don't know why.

MALCOLM. Do you mind that I'm still hanging out with him?

JUDE. No, on the contrary. You should absolutely still be friends with him.

MALCOLM. Even after what he did to you?

JUDE. I don't want him to be abandoned. This is just between us.

WILLEM. Jude, a package arrived.

JUDE (*to himself*). I know what it is.

WILLEM. *Jude, After Sickness*.

JB. I wrote something on the back.

JUDE. 'To Jude: With love and apologies.'

WILLEM. What are you going to do with it?

JUDE. I don't know.

WILLEM. Why don't you give it to Harold? I'm sure he'd love it.

JUDE. No—I have a better idea.

'JB—thanks for the painting, and for your apology, both of which mean a lot. Call me when you have time to hang out. I've missed you, and want to hear what's been going on in your life. P.S. I'm going to donate the painting to MoMA.'

When I was twenty, I would look at my friends and feel such a deep contentment that I would wish the world around us would simply cease, that none of us would have to move from that moment, when everything was in balance.

But now I know that these people I trust might someday betray me.

JB: I'm sorry.

JB and JUDE embrace each other.

JB. We've got to make that party.

MALCOLM. Do we have to, JB?

JB. *Yes*, we have to.

WILLEM. JB, we're thirty-seven. And yet you keep dragging us to your parties.

JB. If you hate them so much, then why do you always come along?

MALCOLM. I'm just happy for the four of us to be together.

WILLEM. At times I feel there's something so pointless about what I do. JB's friends certainly think so—they think I'm a huge sell-out.

JUDE. Well, ever since I left the US Attorney's office and joined Rosen and Pritchard, they think I'm basically an arms dealer. One of JB's friends asked me how it felt waking up every morning knowing I'd sacrificed another piece of my soul the day before by defending white-collar criminals.

MALCOLM. And what has Harold said about your defection?

A change of scene.

HAROLD. I can't say I support this, Jude. You were doing work that really matters. Now you're going to spend your days defending criminals: Liars. Crooks. Thieves. People so entitled they think laws only apply to people of certain races, or to people who earn less than nine figures a year. And for what? Money.

MALCOLM. It's easy for you to have principles, Harold. But we all need money. Even I know that.

Part II 27

HAROLD. A society cannot run fairly if great legal minds don't make it their business to ensure it runs for *everybody*, not just a small group.

JUDE. You're so angry.

HAROLD. I'm disappointed. You could have been a judge.

Anyway, if you needed money, why didn't you come to me?

JUDE. Harold. That's so—generous of you. But—

HAROLD. What do you need all that money for, anyway? You can tell me.

JUDE. How can I tell him that the money I need isn't the money he has? How can I tell him that I dream not of marriage, or children, but of having enough money to pay someone to take care of me when I'm old, someone who'll be kind to me and allow me my dignity? How can I tell him of my deepest fears—of becoming an old man with a catheter, alone in his apartment without an elevator, with no one to help him?

(*To* HAROLD.) I enjoy it.

HAROLD. You enjoy helping huge conglomerates avoid prosecution for fraud? You enjoy working at the margins of corruption?

JUDE. No—it's that I like to explore the elasticity of the law, to stretch it just past its natural tension point.

But the main thing, the thing I cannot tell Harold, is that at Rosen and Pritchard, I have no history. There, I am a series of numbers: one number for how much I earn, another for how many hours I bill; a third for how many people I oversee. I could be anyone; I could be no one at all.

HAROLD. Jude, I've known you for almost a decade now. You're a friend.

But I think of you as much more than that.

JUDE (*silence*).

HAROLD. I want to ask you something. Something—strange. I prepared what to say, but…I'm more nervous than I thought I'd be. I'm wondering if…you might consider… letting me…well, adopt you.

JUDE. But Harold…

HAROLD. Wait. If you say yes, you'd be my legal son, and my legal heir. And if you don't want to, for whatever reason, I understand completely. It won't change how I feel about you, and you're always welcome here.

JUDE. Harold…

HAROLD. Do you want to think about it?

JUDE. I don't need to think about it. There's nothing I've ever wanted more. I just never thought—

HAROLD. You never thought what?

JUDE. Are you sure?

HAROLD. I'm as sure as you are. You?

JUDE. Very sure. You?

HAROLD. Yes.

A change of scene.

MALCOLM. Jude, that's amazing!

WILLEM. How do you feel?

JUDE. Like I'm going to mess it up. (*Pause.*) I've wanted this for so long. My entire life.

WILLEM. You're not going to mess it up.

MALCOLM. Of course you won't, Jude. Do you get a new birth certificate and everything?

JUDE. Yes—yes, I will.

> ANDY *bursts into a series of seal-like sounds, half barking, half sneezing. He is crying.*

> Andy, what's wrong?

ANDY. Get out of here. I mean it, Jude. Get out of here.

JB. Will you take Harold's name? When is this happening? What happens if he gets sick—are you expected to take care of him?

JUDE. JB—I don't know.

JUDE (*reading a letter*). 'Dear Jude, please forgive me. I couldn't be happier for you. The only question is, what took Harold so fucking long? Take this as a sign that you need to take better care of yourself so you can change Harold's adult diapers when he's really old. He won't make it easy for you by dying at a respectable age. Parents are pains in the ass like that (but great, too). Love, Andy.'

WILLEM. No one deserves it more than you. Jude…

JUDE. What?

WILLEM. I love you.

HAROLD. You realize you're going to be bound to me for life?

JUDE. I'm happy to be bound to you for life. (*Pause.*) Harold, I'm tired. Can I go to bed?

6.

ANA. You have to learn to talk about it.

JUDE. Go away.

ANA. It gets harder the longer you wait.

JUDE. I can't.

ANA. It's going to fester inside you, and you'll always think you're to blame. You'll be wrong, but that's what you'll think. But Jude — no matter what you think, you have nothing to be ashamed of, and none of it has been your fault. Can you remember that?

A change of scene.

JUDE. Six weeks until the adoption. Five weeks until the adoption. Four. Willem isn't here with me. I wait for the nights to pass, for the sky to lighten.

I'm thirteen. An adoption fair. A huge room filled with kids. Boys to the left, girls to the right. Tables with stacks of binders. A couple chooses me to spend a weekend with them. 'We want someone hard-working. Someone who appreciates what a home and a house means.' They think my name's a bit unusual. 'We'll call you Cody, is that okay?' 'I like Cody,' I say — Cody, Jude, it makes no difference to me. I enter the house as one person and transform into another. Gone are Brother Luke and the others. Now I am Cody. Cody is a boy with parents, a room of his own. He will be able to make himself into whomever he chooses. But after that weekend I never hear from them again. What did I do wrong? I allowed myself to believe that I might be someone I knew I wasn't.

A change of scene.

ANDY. What should we talk about first? Your extreme weight loss or your excessive cutting?

How much longer until the big day?

JUDE. Three weeks.

ANDY. Why is it so hard?

JUDE. I'm worried—I'm worried that if Harold finds out what I really am…

ANDY. Jude, what's so bad that Harold wouldn't want to adopt you?

JUDE. Don't make me say it, Andy, please.

ANDY. But I honestly don't know!

JUDE. The things I've done. The diseases I got because of what I did.

ANDY. Jude. You were a kid—a baby. Those things were done *to* you. You have nothing, *nothing* to blame yourself for, not ever. And even if you *had* been just some horny guy, not a kid, who wanted to fuck everything in sight, it still wouldn't be anything to be ashamed of.

JUDE. I don't know.

ANDY. Why don't you believe me?

JUDE. I don't know.

ANDY. When you wake up at night and want to cut yourself, I want you to call me. I don't care what time it is, you call me, okay? I mean it.

JUDE. I'm sorry, Andy.

ANDY. You don't need to be sorry—not to me, anyway.

JUDE. To Harold.

ANDY. No. Just to yourself.

> JUDE *goes home. It's night. He cuts himself. The phone rings. It is* ANDY.

Am I calling too late?

JUDE. I'm sorry, Andy.

ANDY. Aren't you tired of this? You don't have to do this to yourself.

> ANDY *calls* WILLEM.

WILLEM. Andy?

ANDY. Where are you? And don't you dare say 'On a shoot.'

WILLEM. Hold on. I *am* on a shoot.

ANDY. He's sitting at home fucking cutting himself to shreds, he's all scar tissue now. He looks like a fucking skeleton, and where are you?

WILLEM. Wait a minute—I call him *every single day*.

ANDY. You *knew* the adoption was going to be hard for him. So why aren't you and his other so-called friends doing anything?

WILLEM. Don't you fucking yell at me, Andy. You're just mad because you can't figure out how to make him better.

Silence.

ANDY. You're right. I'm sorry. But he's had such a shitty life. And he trusts you.

WILLEM. I know that he trusts me. But my job is to treat him as he wants to be treated.

ANDY. I understand, but in the meantime…

WILLEM. What Jude and I have is something, but it's not friendship. I sometimes feel he's a magician, and his sole trick is concealment, and he's so good at it. But how can you help someone who won't be helped, while knowing that if you *don't* try, you're not being a good friend?

We are two people who remain together, day after day, bound not by sex or attraction or law, not by money or children or property, but by the agreement to witness each other's slow drip of miseries, our occasional triumphs. To be present at his dismal moments, and knowing that I can be dismal around him in return. *Talk to me*, I want to tell him. *Tell me things*. How you lived before I met you; anything. But talk to me: I can't figure it out on my own.

7.

BROTHER LUKE. We did it, Jude. We're safe. We'll stay here until I'm sure the other brothers haven't followed us.

Look, two beds. I promised you. You get to choose which one you want. Every morning, we'll take a run, and then I'll teach you: history, math, music, languages.

I'll be gone nights—but I'll always come back. And when I'm gone, don't open the door for anyone. I know you don't want me to go, but I have to find land for our cabin. It'll be in a forest, surrounded by cedars and pines, and behind the cabin we'll have a little stream.

And yet sometimes—I get so sad. I worry that we'll never get it—our cabin. That we'll never have enough money.

JUDE. I want to help. Please let me help you, Brother Luke.

I know how to do a lot of things: I know how to clean, how to iron, I know how to cook. I can peel potatoes. I can mix fertilizer, I know how to add eggshells to the soil. I can do anything you want.

BROTHER LUKE. Jude, Jude—I know you want to help. And you will.

In a few minutes, a man will come in. You're going to do with him what you did with Father Gabriel and the other brothers.

It'll be over so fast, I promise you. And I'll be waiting in the bathroom to make sure nothing goes wrong.

Jude, it's because of you that we'll get our cabin.

8.

JUDE. I don't want to tell you this, Harold, but I have to…
I think you see me as…as someone I'm not. You see me as a good person. Someone decent.

HAROLD. Yes, I do.

ANA. Is it so hard for you to believe that someone wants you?

JUDE. What if I wake up one day and Harold's gone?

ANA. So you'd prefer he doesn't adopt you at all?

JUDE. Yes. No. I don't know. I just know I'll look back one day when it's over and know that I caused it.

(*To* HAROLD.) I've done bad things, things I'm ashamed of. If you knew, you'd be ashamed to know me, let alone be related to me.

Silence.

HAROLD. Jude St Francis, as your future parent, I hereby absolve you of everything for which you seek absolution.

HAROLD *takes off his watch, gives it to* JUDE.

My father gave this to me when I turned thirty. Now you're thirty, so…

JUDE. There are three sets of initials engraved on the back.

HAROLD. Saul Stein. My father.

JUDE. Harold Stein.

HAROLD. Me.

JUDE. Jude St Francis.

HAROLD. You.

JUDE. I can't accept this.

HAROLD. You can't refuse it.

JUDE. I have something for you, too.

JUDE *sings an early song by Schubert. While he's singing, the others arrive to the party.*

HAROLD. JB and Malcolm, welcome! Though it's a pity Willem can't be here.

MALCOLM. Well, he's on a shoot.

JB. Harold! Congratulations! It's a boy!

MALCOLM. I'm sure he hasn't heard *that* one before.

WILLEM *arrives unexpectedly.*

WILLEM. Congratulations!

JUDE. Willem! You're here!

WILLEM. Was it that hard without me?

JUDE. It wasn't great. But it wasn't horrible, either.

WILLEM. I wish I could have been there.

JUDE. I missed you.

WILLEM. I missed you, too.

JUDE. I'm someone's son.

WILLEM. Yes, you're someone's son.

JUDE. Do you think it went all right?

WILLEM. Are you kidding? Did you see Harold's face? Jude, he loves you.

JUDE. Tell me again.

WILLEM. He loves you.

p. 1 *Jude, After Sickness*
p. 2 *Malcolm and His Father*
p. 3 *Willem Before Auditioning*
p. 4 *Jude at the Theater*

All paintings by Eniwaye Oluwaseyi
Courtesy of Zidoun-Bossuyt Gallery

Part III

1.

JB. Okay, yes. I did a bad thing. I gave my word to Jude and I broke it. Willem took Jude's side, and though they said they forgave me, they never really did. And now it's Jude and Willem, united against the world—and me. They needed me once—they were the boring ones and *they* needed *me*. But now that they're successful, I guess they don't any longer (even though they're still boring). And *that's* why I get high: Not for the escape from everyday life, but because it makes everyday life seem less everyday. It convinces me that the world is splendid and unknown. We were so much more fun back then.

(*To* JUDE.) Do you want to just spend your life being completely average and boring and typical?

JUDE. Actually, JB, that's in fact exactly what I want.

JB. What, you just want to play house with Harold your whole life?

JUDE. That too, yes.

JB. But we're invited on Jackson's yacht!

JUDE. But it's Thanksgiving. I always go to Harold's for Thanksgiving. You know that.

JB. Well, what about Willem?

JUDE. You'll have to ask him.

JB. But if you say no, Willem will too. So Malcolm and I'll have to go to Harold's, too, and have the most boring Thanksgiving imaginable: mediocre food; liberals shouting about issues they *all agree on*. I could be on that boat with Jackson and his friends—not that I even like them. And I hate their work. They say Jackson's mother buys out his shows so it makes it look like he's in demand. We were out once, and Jackson buys two candy bars with a hundred-dollar bill and said 'keep the change,' just slapping the money down on the counter. I know there's something obscene about it. But it's also exciting—it reminds me how conventional my friends are, how bourgeois.

JB *gets a panic attack.* JUDE, WILLEM *and* MALCOLM *stand next to him.*

JB. Jackson?

MALCOLM. It's us.

JB. Jude, aren't you going to lecture me?

JUDE. No.

JB. Don't go!

JUDE. I'm not going anywhere.

JB. Where's Willem? Where is he?

JUDE. Willem's here, too.

JB. Why aren't we friends anymore, Willem?

WILLEM. We *are* friends, JB. You know I love you.

MALCOLM. We're getting you out of here.

JB. No. I can't. Don't make me.

WILLEM. You're coming. And that's it.

JB. No—wait. *Stop.* You can't just barge in here and make a fool of me: Oh, I'm Willem the Hero, I'm here to save JB the Fuck-up, just like always, while you and Jude give each other side-eye and think I don't notice. But I do—I see it all.

(*To* JUDE.) And you, Jude? You like being the person who knows everyone else's secrets, without ever telling us a fucking thing? Well, it doesn't work that way, and we're all fucking sick of you.

WILLEM. That's enough, JB.

JB. It doesn't work like that!

Then, as if on impulse, JB *does an impersonation of* JUDE. *He lets his mouth hang open, wails like an imbecile, and drags his right leg as if it were made of stone.*

I'm Jude. I'm Jude St Francis.

WILLEM *knocks him to the ground.*

Oh god. Oh god. What have I done?

I'm sorry, Jude.

I'm sorry. I'm so sorry.

Forgive me.

Forgive me.

Forgive me.

Part IV

It is three years later. JB *is clean.* JUDE *still hasn't forgiven him, and* WILLEM *has also distanced himself. Only* MALCOLM *still hangs out with* JB.

1.

MALCOLM *comes by with the drawings of Greene Street.*

MALCOLM. The blueprints for Greene Street. Want to see them?

JUDE. Why are there no doors?

MALCOLM. It's a loft, Jude. You should respect it.

JUDE. Malcolm. I need a bedroom. With a door that I can close and lock. And what's this?

MALCOLM. Grab bars. Jude, I know what you are going to say, but...

JUDE. And this? Steel bars in the bathroom? But Malcolm— I'm not in a wheelchair right now.

MALCOLM. But Jude...

JUDE. I don't want a cripple's apartment.

MALCOLM. It's not. It's just as a precaution—

JUDE. Get rid of them. I don't want them. I'm forty, not eighty.

MALCOLM. But as a matter of practicality—

JUDE. Malcolm. No.

MALCOLM. Okay, Jude, okay—I understand. Counters back up to standard height. No grab bars in the shower, but I'll install a bench instead, and I swear it'll look nice. But Jude—I'm going to keep the grab bars around the toilet. We'll install them last, and if you hate them, we'll leave them off. Just think about it, okay?

A change of scene.

JB. Will we ever make up, Jude?

JUDE. I don't know.

JB. I love you, you know that. I would never intentionally hurt you, never.

JUDE. I know, JB. I know.

JB. I want to tell you—completely sober—that I'm so sorry. It was horrible. I'm sorry. Please say that you forgive me.

JUDE. Just those few words—

ANA. I forgive you…

JUDE. I can't say it.

JB. Don't you think I love you?

JUDE. I know you do.

JB. You do?

JUDE. I remember one time, years ago, in Harold's kitchen. You were sketching. And from your expression I knew you were drawing something special, something that was dear to you. I asked, *What are you drawing?* And you said…

JB. I'm drawing you. Always.

JUDE. Oh, JB, I miss you. I *will* miss you.

JB. But you can't forgive me?

JUDE. I can't look at you without seeing...I'm sorry.

JB. Oh.

JUDE. JB. I only want great things for you.

JB. Well.

> JB *leaves*.

JUDE. JB's right. 'I'm Jude St Francis...'

> (*To* WILLEM.) Willem, can I ask you something? Is JB right? Do I not tell you enough about myself?

WILLEM. You don't owe me your secrets, Jude. But—a friend of mine recently asked me if you were gay or straight, and I had to tell her I didn't know. She was shocked. She said, this is your best friend since you guys were teenagers, and you don't know?

JUDE (*silence*).

WILLEM. So, yes. This is the kind of stuff I wish you'd tell me. Maybe you're both. Maybe you're neither. It doesn't make a difference to me.

JUDE (*silence*).

WILLEM. Jude, do you want to be with someone?

JUDE. That's not for someone like me.

WILLEM. But that's not what I asked.

JUDE. I'm tired, Willem. I need to go to bed.

WILLEM. Jude, don't walk away from me. I'm trying to talk to you about something important.

JUDE. You're right. I'm sorry. But this is just too difficult for me to discuss.

WILLEM. *Everything's* too difficult for you to discuss.
I'm sorry. But, Jude—are you ever lonely?

JUDE. No.

WILLEM. I don't believe you.

JUDE. Willem, you have to stop worrying. I'm always going to be able to take care of myself.

WILLEM. You always say that.

JUDE. Because it's always true.

HAROLD. This is a terrific place, Jude. Malcolm did such a good job. It's massive, though. Don't you get lonely in here by yourself?

JUDE. No, Harold, I'm fine.

HAROLD. Well, what about me? I'd like to see you with someone.

JUDE. Last time I checked, it wasn't against the law to be single, Harold.

HAROLD. Sorry, Jude, I just thought…

JUDE. I'm sorry, Harold. I didn't mean to snap at you. I'll think about it. I promise.

Once HAROLD *is gone,* JUDE *undresses on the way to the bathroom. Shoes, sweater, shirt, pants. His hands tremble as he takes the bag from under the sink. He makes new cuts over old ones, sawing through the scar tissue with the edge of the blade. He sees with disgust, horror and fascination how badly he has deformed himself. When he's done, he washes the blood away carefully.*

BROTHER LUKE. Jude: My sleepyhead. My dreamer. I know you're tired. It's normal: you're growing. It's tiring, growing up. And I know you work hard. But when you're with your clients, you have to show a little life. They're paying to be with you; you have to show them you're enjoying it.

You were made for this, Jude. It's okay to enjoy it.

Why don't you give me one of your smiles?

JUDE. In Texas, I had a client: covered in eczema, his stomach drooping between his legs. As I gave him a blowjob, the man's gut pressed against my neck, and the man cried. *I'm sorry, I'm sorry*, he kept repeating, dragging the tips of his fingers across my scalp, as if they were a comb, *I'm sorry*.

I sometimes fear I am that man.

ANA. And so you choose to be lonely.

JUDE. Loneliness isn't fatal.

WILLEM. I have to go away again, Jude.

JUDE. Will you take care of yourself?

WILLEM. Yes.

BROTHER LUKE. Smiley face, do you love me?

JUDE. Yes.

BROTHER LUKE. Come. Your next client.

2.

CALEB. Caleb Porter.

JUDE. Jude St Francis.

CALEB. Let me guess: Catholic.

JUDE. Let *me* guess: not.

CALEB. You'd be right about that.

Should I keep going?

JUDE. Maybe...

CALEB. Forty-nine. Went to law school. Never used what I learned there. I'm the CEO of a fashion label—it's a nightmare. Do you know any designers?

JUDE. No. But I know a lot of artists.

CALEB. Well. So you understand. They're incapable of meeting deadlines and staying within budget.

JUDE. Oh, yes, that *does* sound familiar. So how do you manage them?

CALEB. What you have to do is present the rules of business like bylaws of their own small universe—if they don't follow them, their universe collapses.

JUDE. So why do you do it?

CALEB. Sometimes I don't know. But then you watch them sketch or drape or just put colors together, and it's—it's wondrous.

JUDE. I know exactly what you mean.

CALEB. Are you single?

Why are you looking at me like that?

JUDE. Sorry. Yes, I'm single. I have to go.

CALEB. I'll walk with you.

JUDE. You don't mind?

CALEB. Not at all.

At the apartment.

Without waiting for JUDE*'s answer,* CALEB *kisses him. He pushes* JUDE *against the door and uses his arms to form a cage around him.*

JUDE. I thought you were looking for legal representation.

CALEB. No. (*Pause.*) Aren't you going to invite me up?

ANA. Jude…

JUDE. He's asking if I'm going to invite him up.

ANA. Jude…

JUDE (*to* CALEB). Let's go.

JUDE *walks in front of* CALEB.

CALEB. When I met you, I didn't know you had a limp.

JUDE. That's true. Would you not have talked to me if you'd known?

CALEB. I don't know. (*Sees the wheelchair.*) Whose wheelchair is that?

JUDE. Mine.

CALEB. But why?

JUDE. Sometimes I need it. Rarely.

CALEB. I hope so.

JUDE (*silence*).

CALEB. Sorry. I know it must seem bizarre to you, but I have a real aversion to wheelchairs.

ANA. Jude…

JUDE. It doesn't seem bizarre at all. I do, too.

CALEB. My father had MS. My mother had face pains, headaches. And though I don't doubt it was real, it bothered me — it was as if they didn't *want* to get better. As if they just surrendered to illness: first canes, then walkers, then wheelchairs, and vials of pills, pain creams, gels, and then more and more.

ANA. You must send him away, now.

CALEB. I want to see you again, but not around these — these *instruments* of disease. It makes me feel furious, like I need to fight against it. Do you understand what I mean?

ANA. You must send him away, now.

JUDE. Yes. I feel the same way.

ANA. There's a fairy tale: a woman lives on the edge of a dark forest in a little wooden cabin. One night, she hears a knock, and she opens the door. She doesn't see anyone, but in those few seconds, dozens of creatures — monsters, goblins — slip into her house. And once they're inside, she will never be able to make them leave. Never.

JUDE. We have to go slowly.

CALEB. Why?

JUDE. It's been a long time.

CALEB. How long?

JUDE. Long.

CALEB. Take off your clothes.

JUDE. No.

CALEB. Why not?

JUDE. I can't, Caleb. I don't want you to see me.

CALEB. Why not?

JUDE. I have scars. On my back, legs and arms. I don't want you to see them. They're disgusting. You won't like them.

CALEB. Well. I don't need to see all of your body, do I? Just the relevant parts.

They have sex.

JUDE. It's worse than I expected, worse than I'd remembered. I'd forgotten how painful and disgusting it is, and being half-dressed is somehow much worse than being told to take everything off.

And yet things are also not completely horrible. I like Caleb's slow way of speaking. I like how, like Willem, he's so at ease in his body. I like his solidity, his physical strength. I like how in his sleep he slings an arm across my chest, how he carries a faint threat of danger, how when he's leaving, he'll put his hands on my face and hold them there for a moment.

A change of scene.

CALEB. Why are you walking like that?

JUDE. Am I walking strangely?

CALEB. Yeah.

ANA. Leave. Leave now.

JUDE. I wasn't aware of it.

CALEB. Well, stop it. It looks ridiculous.

JUDE. It's nerve damage. It's out of my control—I can't help it.

JUDE *tries to walk normally. He falls.* CALEB *hits him in the face.*

CALEB. I'm sorry, Jude. Your poor face.

CALEB *takes* JUDE's *face in his hands.*

ANA. Send him away.

CALEB. Your poor face.

JUDE. I'm not sure whether I can do this.

CALEB. I just want to stay with you a bit.

ANA. Caleb doesn't force him to have sex, so he sleeps well. The next morning, he wakes up.

JUDE *tries to walk. He falls.*

JUDE. I'm sorry, it's my fault. I'm sorry, Caleb.

CALEB. Get up! Get up!

ANA. Tell him it's over.

Caleb picks up a bottle of wine and hits you in the neck with it.

JUDE. Caleb, please, please. I beg you. Forgive me. I'm sorry. I'm sorry.

CALEB. Get up *now*.

JUDE. It's my fault.

Please, Caleb. Don't. Please.

CALEB *rapes* JUDE. CALEB *leaves the stage, slams the door.*

ANA. Jude. Why would you be with someone who treats you like that?

JUDE. I was lonely. And now the worst has happened. I was in a relationship and it was horrible. But now it's over.

CALEB *returns.*

ANA. Three weeks later.

CALEB. Jude.

JUDE. Caleb—

CALEB. I have a key, you know.

JUDE. Please go. Please, Caleb.

CALEB. Undress.

JUDE. I don't want to.

> *As* CALEB *takes off* JUDE*'s clothes,* JUDE *struggles, yelling out for* CALEB *to stop. When* CALEB*'s taken off all of* JUDE*'s clothes, he steps back, appraises him.*

CALEB. My god. You really are deformed.

ANA. Remember how you were able to leave your body as a child. You'd pretend to be a thing without a soul, like a ceiling fan. You'd float above the room, you'd watch the scene beneath you and not feel a thing.

CALEB. Come here.

JUDE. What're you going to do?

CALEB. We're going outside.

JUDE. No. No!—Caleb. No!

CALEB. Ask me to stay with you. Beg me.

JUDE. Stay with me.

CALEB. Apologize to me.

JUDE. I'm sorry, Caleb; I'm so sorry.

CALEB. Repeat after me: I'm repulsive.

JUDE. I'm repulsive.

CALEB. I'm disgusting.

JUDE. I'm disgusting.

CALEB. I'm worthless.

JUDE. I'm worthless.

CALEB. I'm sorry.

JUDE. I'm sorry. I'm sorry. I'm sorry.

> CALEB *pushes him back inside.*

My beautiful apartment. These beautiful floors that Malcolm thought of for me. The only place I ever felt safe.

CALEB. What's behind this door? It's the fire escape.

JUDE. I know what's going to happen next. It's inevitable. It's the Axiom of Equality, my favorite mathematical axiom, in which X always equals X — no matter what.

CALEB. You may live in this apartment you love, you may have a job you love, you have a father and friends who love you. You may be respected; in court, even feared. But fundamentally…

JUDE. …I remain the same person.

ANA. Caleb rushes at you, kicks you in your back, and you go flying into the fire escape, down its stairs.

JUDE. X equals X. X equals X.

ANA. It is the last thing you think before crashing onto the concrete.

3.

HAROLD. I had a son before him: Jacob. I was thirty-two when he was born, thirty-six when he was diagnosed, thirty-seven when he died. It began when a teacher saw him sleeping in a corner of the classroom, while the other children were in a jumble, talking and jumping. Things were all right for a while. And then one day—it was dinnertime—he began seizing. He was rigid, his body becoming a plank, his eyeballs rolling upward, his throat making an odd, clicking noise, so awful and specific that I can still hear it.

We got the best neurologist, the best geneticist, the best immunologist. He had all kinds of tests: blood, brain, reflexes, hearing. By the time we had the diagnosis—Nishihara syndrome: an extremely rare neurodegenerative disease—he was almost blind. He had stopped growing. When I held him, I had to make sure to hold his arms against his body, or they would dangle off of him and he would look dead.

My father had always said that the hardest thing about being a parent is recalibration. The better you are at it, the better you will be. When we first realized that Jacob was sick, we tried very hard to recalibrate. We all *say* we want our kids to be happy, only happy, and healthy, but we don't want that. We want them to be like we are, or better than we are.

But the point of a child is not what you hope he will accomplish, but the pleasure that he will bring you, in whatever form it comes, even if it is a form that is barely recognizable as pleasure at all. And, more importantly, the pleasure you will be privileged to bring him.

HAROLD *visits* JUDE. *He finds* JUDE *badly injured on the ground.*

JUDE. I'm sorry, Harold. I'm so sorry.

HAROLD *carries* JUDE *to* ANDY.

ANDY. Broken left wrist, four broken ribs. No concussion, thank god. Bruising all up and down his face. Eyes and nose are fine. Lacerations on his legs. This is what I'm worried about.

Fractured coccyx. Dislocated shoulder. No internal bleeding, fortunately. But look at his back.

HAROLD. What is that?

ANDY. He was probably whipped with a belt. I want to find that fuck and kill him.

HAROLD. Me too.

> HAROLD *brings* JUDE *back to his apartment on Greene Street.*

JUDE. You cleaned.

HAROLD. Well, yes. Not as well as you would have.

JUDE. Thank you, Harold.

HAROLD. Jude, can I ask you something?

Did — did someone do something to you when you were a child?

JUDE. Jesus, Harold.

HAROLD. How old were you when it happened?

JUDE. Harold. I'm tired. I need to go to bed.

HAROLD. You know that guy is a fucking asshole, right? You know you're wrong about yourself, right?

You said, 'When you look like I do, you take what you can get.' How can I call myself a father if my child thinks that about himself?

> JUDE *doesn't answer.*

JUDE. They call them 'examinations.' Afternoons with Brother Peter, evenings with Father Gabriel. I throw myself against walls and scream as loudly as I can. *You're a monster*, they say. But I can't control it. It's like there's something ferocious inside of me, and I know that they're frightened when I scream like this. They fear me, my noise and power. But I fear myself, too. At times I lose consciousness when they hit me, but I come to crave it: It helps me control the beast—I can't do it alone.

ANA. Then the bed-wetting starts.

JUDE. The more examinations the Father gives me, the more I wet the bed. I know I stink, of urine and blood. Once, both Father Gabriel and Brother Peter are in my room. I'm trying not to scream. The quieter I am, the sooner it will end. And then, quick as a moth, I see Brother Luke passing outside my door. *Brother Luke!* But he doesn't stop, and I feel myself fill with rage. Afterward, I go to the greenhouse and snap off every one of the daffodils' heads.

When I return to my room, the door is shut. I wait, and then I fling it open. But there's no one there—just a glass jar with white hyacinths. I want to tear at myself from grief.

HAROLD. You didn't do anything wrong. You know that, right? You know you're not to blame, right? That this isn't your fault? You know that this says nothing about you and what you're worth.

BROTHER LUKE. Don't cry.

JUDE. I ruined Brother Luke's flowers, the only one who never hurt me.

BROTHER LUKE. Don't cry.

JUDE. To the other brothers, I'm a burden, a collection of problems.

BROTHER LUKE. Come, I have something to show you.

JUDE. But to Brother Luke, I'm someone else: someone smart and funny. Someone to be around.

BROTHER LUKE. Come sit next to me. I know you like it here, in the greenhouse. It's so peaceful, isn't it?

ANA. Was that the moment?

JUDE (*silence*).

ANA. The moment when you later knew: *This is when it happened, this is where it started.*

JUDE (*silence*).

ANA. The moment you gave up everything to follow Brother Luke.

JUDE. That was the moment.

BROTHER LUKE. Here, Jude, this is for you.

JUDE. What is it?

BROTHER LUKE. It's a birthday cake. It's not every day you turn eight, is it?

Go on, blow them out.

Jude, do you like it here?

JUDE. I'd like to spend my whole life here.

BROTHER LUKE. Jude, what they do with you, it isn't right. They shouldn't be hurting you like they do.

I look at you and I think: You don't deserve what happens to you. You deserve to be with someone else.

HAROLD. Jude…

JUDE. Please, Harold, don't.

HAROLD. It's not your fault, do you understand? It's not your fault.

BROTHER LUKE. I had a son once. I loved him so much. You remind me so much of him. But then he died, and I came to the monastery.

Jude, you know I would never hurt you, right? If we were together, we'd have such a wonderful time. I'd teach you how to fish. We'd live in a little cabin in the woods, like a father and son. We'd grow vegetables in our garden, flowers, too. You want to grow pumpkins, right? And you know what, Jude? You'd have your own bed. A real bed.

But thinking about this makes me very sad.

JUDE. Why?

BROTHER LUKE. Because even though I care so much about you, I feel that you don't care about me.

JUDE. No, that's not true, Brother Luke!

BROTHER LUKE. I talk about our house in the forest. But do you really want to go there? Or are they just stories to you, like fairy tales?

JUDE. No, they're not just fairy tales.

BROTHER LUKE. Would you do anything to make this all come true? To build our house? To have it be just the two of us in our small and perfect world?

JUDE. Yes, Brother Luke—I'd do anything.

BROTHER LUKE. Do you want me, like I want you?

JUDE. Yes.

BROTHER LUKE. Are you ready to go?

JUDE. Yes—yes, I'm ready.

BROTHER LUKE. Oh, Jude. I'm so glad I picked you.

HAROLD, *as if* JUDE *were a wild animal, slowly raises his hand…*

JUDE. Don't touch me!

...and strokes JUDE *on the back of his head twice.*

HAROLD. I'm sorry.

JUDE. I'm really tired. I need to sleep.

4.

ANA. When he opened his eyes in the hospital after the crash, he saw me first. *Well, well*, I said. *He awakes.* He couldn't remember who he was, or what had happened. I stayed with him when he woke up screaming. To him it was neither day or night. But he'd see me, remember where he was, and close his eyes again. I'd ask him if he was hungry — I had a sandwich for him no matter his answer. I asked him if he was in pain.

First, there were the wounds on his legs: His vascular system had been so compromised, the doctor said, that he might have open sores on them for years. *How long*, I asked. *Forever*, he said.

Then there were the episodes with his back. He talked about the painful jabs that preceded them, fierce and zingy, a sensation of electric prickles moving up and down his spine. I was there when he had his first one — as if someone reached in and grabbed his spine like a snake and was trying to loosen it from its bundles of nerves by shaking it. When the surgeon said he'd have these episodes all his life, I was furious.

He was too tired and frightened to fight with me, and after a while, he allowed me to hold his hand when was in pain. He held it so tightly that I could feel every bone in my palm reposition itself in his grip.

JUDE. 'Count to a hundred.'

ANA. And again.

JUDE. 'And again.'

ANA. When the worst of the pain was over, I would give him some water, a straw in the glass so he wouldn't have to raise his head.

JUDE. 'It'll get better, Jude. It won't hurt as much next time.'

ANA *starts to cry uncontrollably.*

Ana?

ANA. I took him to most of his doctors' appointments. I was there when he took his first slow steps. I knew he was smart. I found him a tutor when he couldn't go to high school. I discussed college with him.

It took me a month before I asked: *Can you tell me what happened?*

JUDE. I don't remember anything.

ANA. You're lying.

JUDE. What do you mean?

ANA. You won't remember, but you woke up soon after surgery. You were lucid, and I asked questions and you answered them.

JUDE. About what happened that night?

ANA. Yes, and the years before, as well.

JUDE. How much did I tell you?

ANA. Enough to convince me that there's a hell and those men should be in it.

JUDE. You're angry.

ANA. I am, yes. But not with you.

JUDE. Ana, you shouldn't have done it.

ANA. I was very sick. You couldn't see it, because you were so sick as well.

JUDE. You convinced me to keep living, and then you died yourself.

ANA. You have friends…

JUDE. They want things from me. They ask me what happened to my legs and back, why I don't want to be touched.

ANA. I can teach you.

JUDE. What?

ANA. To talk about it. About what happened. What it did to you.

JUDE. Ana, how could you let me believe I might be equipped to do this? Why did you never tell me how ugly my life really was?

Part V

1.

JUDE. Yes, go away. I'll do this on my own.

It's taking so much time, so much effort to forget my months with Caleb. And complicating it is Harold, who keeps asking me questions.

HAROLD. How are you? How do you feel? How are your legs? Are you using the chair a lot? Do you need help with anything?

JUDE. No, Harold, I'm fine. I'm fine!

JUDE throws himself against the wall.

BROTHER LUKE. Jude, Jude, what are you doing?! You know the clients don't like seeing you all bruised.

JUDE. The months with Caleb are like hyenas: every day, they chase me. I run from them, but the things that helped me before don't help anymore. Cleaning doesn't help, or cooking. I recite proofs, and case law, but they won't go away. I cut and I cut, but they won't go away.

ANDY. I want you to see a psychologist.

JUDE. I'm fine. I can help myself.

ANDY. And how are you going to do that, help yourself?

BROTHER LUKE. I want to teach you a secret. Something better than throwing yourself against walls.

ANDY. By cutting yourself?

BROTHER LUKE. Here: razors, alcohol wipes, cotton, and bandages. You'll see what feels best.

JUDE. I can be at the movies with Willem or cooking, and suddenly, a scene appears of the years with Brother Luke, the months with Dr Traylor, a scene from the crash, the glow of the headlights, my head jerking to one side.

BROTHER LUKE. It'll drain away the rage inside you.

WILLEM. Jude. Are you okay?

JUDE. It's like Caleb unleashed something inside of me. I can't make it stop, I can't.

WILLEM. What is it, Jude? Your hands are shaking.

JUDE. I want to be alone.

WILLEM. Then we'll be alone together.

JUDE. No, Willem.

WILLEM. Something happened while I was away. Tell me what it is.

JUDE. I can't, Willem, I can't.

WILLEM. I'm staying here tonight.

JUDE. Willem, I...

WILLEM. You get to choose, Jude: either I call Andy or Harold or you let me stay and monitor you — you *at least* owe me that.

JUDE. He stays, and for a while, it helps — the hyenas retreat. But then Willem has to go to work. I want to beg him to stay here with me, but I know I can't.

WILLEM. Are you going to take care of yourself?

JUDE. Yes, Willem. I promise.

JUDE *holds* WILLEM *against him, something he rarely does, and feels that* WILLEM *is surprised at first but then responds, tightening his hold. They stand in a close embrace for a long time.*

BROTHER LUKE. Do you know how much I love you? More than my own self. You're like my own son. Even the clients see it. They ask me: 'Your son is nine? He looks older.' I tell them, 'He's tall for his age.'

WILLEM. Will you really be okay?

JUDE. Yes.

Willem leaves and the hyenas return. I am naked in the rain on Greene Street, I am flying down the stairs, I am being raped in the shower, in the elevator, in the living room. I have a dream in which I'm running across a vast savanna and behind me is a dark cloud that keeps drawing closer and closer. I have to keep running, but I can't keep going forever, and I run and I run and I run.

They're so fast, the hyenas: I know that if they catch me, they'll destroy me. But I'm so tired. And then I hear a voice, unfamiliar, calm and authoritative. *Stop*, it says. *You can end this. You don't have to do this.* I know what it means and yet I stop anyway, and I turn and face the cloud, the hyenas, and wait for them to overwhelm me.

Willem! Help me! I can't stop them, the memories, still so vivid after all these years. Why is it that they grow more powerful as I get older? Brother Luke's scent, the taste of his mouth, its old-coffee tang, his tongue, slippery and skinned trying to burrow inside of me, his voice saying to the clients:

BROTHER LUKE. This is Joey.

JUDE. The feeling that nothing is mine: not my eyes, not my mouth, not even my name. *Joey. Joey.*

WILLEM. Hello, Jude?

JUDE. There is no law stating that I must go on with this. It's my life. I can do with it what I want. I can be my own salvation.

WILLEM. Jude?

JUDE. Hi, Willem. How are you?

WILLEM. You sound better. Lighter.

JUDE. I am.

> JUDE *goes to the bathroom with a glass of whiskey and a box cutter.*

I hope you can forgive me.

He takes off his jacket. Shoes. Tie. Watch. First the left arm. First cut.

BROTHER LUKE. Jude, do you love me?

JUDE. Yes.

> BROTHER LUKE *starts kissing* JUDE, *wraps his arms around him.* JUDE *returns the embrace.*

Around me, on the savanna, the hyenas howl. Before me stands a house with an open door. I am close: close enough to see that inside, there is a bed, a bed where I can rest—at last.

> JUDE *is lying in a pool of blood by the sink.*

> JUDE *is carried to* ANDY's *doctor's bed by* HAROLD, JB, MALCOLM *and* WILLEM.

INTERMISSION

2.

JUDE *lies on the hospital bed.*

JUDE. Andy? Harold? Malcolm? JB? Willem? Aren't you supposed to be in Sri Lanka for a shoot? Willem, you're crying. Why are you crying? You're all crying. I'd like to cry, too — because I haven't been successful. Because I'm still here. Funny, the way everyone looks the same when they cry. Harold? I'm sorry. I failed.

Willem, you're here. What are you reading?

WILLEM. A play I'm thinking of doing.

JUDE. Are you going away again?

WILLEM. No. I thought I'd stick around New York for a while.

JUDE. I realized: I never gave you a present for your birthday. What would you like?

WILLEM. Jude...

JUDE. Yes?

WILLEM. Who's Brother Luke?

JUDE. How — how do you know that name?

WILLEM. At the hospital...in your sleep, you kept shouting: *Help me, Brother Luke.*

JUDE. Ana!

WILLEM. Who's Ana?

JUDE. Nothing.

ANA. I'm here.

JUDE. Teach me how to do it. Teach me how to talk about it.

ANA. You have to start by trusting Willem.

WILLEM. Tell me who Brother Luke is. And not just who he is, but what your—relationship with him was. I want you to tell me the whole story. From start to finish.

JUDE. Part of me wants to. But you're going to be disgusted by me.

ANA. It's time. It's time.

JUDE. I can't say it; I can't find the words.

WILLEM. What about I ask you about something else, then, something easier? And then I'll ask you something else, and something else. And if they're too hard to answer, we'll discuss that, too.

ANA. Willem would never hurt you, never.

WILLEM. What's that scar on your hand?

JUDE. Oh, that. I almost forgot about it. It was a punishment. The brothers thought I'd stolen Father Gabriel's lighter.

WILLEM. Was Brother Luke one of them?

JUDE. I can't, Willem. I can't, I can't. Leave me alone, please.

Part VI

1.

WILLEM. My work, my very life, is one of disguises and charades. But my friendship with Jude makes me feel real, immutable, elemental. It makes me feel that there's something about me that he sees even when I can't, as if his very witness of me makes me real.

Two years after his suicide attempt, I'm sometimes surprised he's still here. I go into his room at odd hours to give myself confirmation that he's there, and alive.

WILLEM *walks into the bedroom and looks at* JUDE, *who is sleeping.*

What would be easier than getting into bed with you and falling asleep?

JUDE *wakes up, as if he senses something.*

JUDE. Willem, are you all right?

WILLEM. What would be simpler than reaching over and kissing you?

JUDE. You know, Willem, it's been a huge gift having you live with me. I don't know what I would have done without you. But you don't have to, you know—I promise you I'll be fine on my own.

WILLEM. But I like being here. Besides, I told Andy I'd keep an eye on you.

JUDE. But you don't have to.

WILLEM. Do you want me to go?

JUDE. No, but I want you to be happy.

WILLEM. I don't know where I'm going, but I know that I'll always make sure that nothing happens to either of us.

Do you understand what I'm trying to say?

JUDE. No.

WILLEM. I'm saying...that I'm attracted to you.

JUDE (*silence*).

WILLEM. I don't think it's that odd. Haven't you felt that way about me over the years?

JUDE. No.

A change of scene.

ANDY. You two always had something special, Willem. So, no. I don't think it's strange at all.

WILLEM. I don't know, Andy. Sometimes I wonder whether what I'm feeling isn't just guilt about his suicide attempt. And other times—I wonder if it wasn't meant to be this way, all along; if I wasn't meant to be with him.

ANDY. Willem...A relationship with you would be the greatest gift he could ever get. But it's going to be very, very tough for him to be intimate with you.

A change of scene.

JUDE. I made a list, and there are at least twenty reasons you shouldn't want to be with me.

WILLEM. Twenty? Wow. That's a lot. Such as?

JUDE. My body.

WILLEM. I hate to tell you this, Jude, but we have the same body.

JUDE. You know what I mean.

WILLEM. Jude. If you don't want this, I'll back off. Nothing will change between us. But if you're scared and self-conscious…I don't think that's a reason not to try. We'll go as slowly as you want, I promise.

JUDE. Can I have a minute?

WILLEM. Of course.

JUDE. Okay.

WILLEM. Come here.

> WILLEM *kisses* JUDE.

JUDE. I'm sorry.

WILLEM. Are you all right?

JUDE. I'm not very good at this.

WILLEM. What do you mean? You're great at it.

JUDE. I think of Brother Luke all the time, his awful tongue, the grain of coffee grounds in his mouth. One of the things I liked about Caleb: He didn't drink coffee.

ANA. Willem is not Brother Luke, or Caleb. He would never hurt you, not ever.

WILLEM. Tell me what you want and what you don't want.

JUDE. I don't like the taste of coffee. I hate it, actually.

WILLEM. Coffee?

Well, that's fine. I just won't drink it.

JUDE. But you love coffee.

WILLEM. I enjoy it, yes. But I don't need it.

JUDE. Do you want to have sex with me someday?

WILLEM. Yes, I'd like to.

JUDE. It's going to take me a while.

WILLEM. That's okay.

JUDE. What if it takes longer?

WILLEM. Then it will.

JUDE. Like months? Or years?

WILLEM. Then it does.

JUDE. But—what are you going to do in the meantime?

WILLEM. This may shock you, Jude, but I am in fact able to go for periods without having sex.

Can I lie down next to you?

JUDE. He tucks his arm under my neck and then across my shoulders, and his other arm around my stomach, moving his legs between my legs. It's a strange sensation, but then I realize I like it. It's like I'm being—

ANA. Swaddled.

WILLEM. Shall we tell the others about us?

JUDE. Yes.

HAROLD. I'm so happy. So happy. I don't know what to say.

MALCOLM. I love the idea of you two together. How long has this been going on?

JB. I'm really happy. I mean. I'm angry that you didn't tell me earlier. But I'm happy. I mean, I'm *really* angry. But. I. Am. Happy.

HAROLD. But Willem, you should know that you can't change your mind. And that I will always pick Jude over you.

JB (*to* WILLEM). So you've always liked Jude more. I knew it. I always have. And maybe it's a tiny bit self-involved, but part of me is miffed that you picked Jude and not me.

WILLEM. JB. I'm not attracted to you. And you aren't attracted to me, either! We made out once, remember? You said it was a huge turn-off!

JB. In ten years I predict both of you will have fully transitioned into lesbiandom. I predict cats.

But I'm really happy for you. I really am. How's the sex?

WILLEM. Amazing.

JB. Damn it.

WILLEM. But I have no idea if the sex is amazing, because we don't have sex.

ANDY. I know it's not easy, but you must be doing something right, Willem. I've never seen him more relaxed or happier, not ever.

2.

JUDE *gets undressed.*

JUDE. Willem.

> JUDE *sleeps.* WILLEM *switches on the nightlight and runs his fingers over* JUDE*'s body. Studies it.*

WILLEM. The inside of your arms, your legs, your back—the skin changing from rough to glossy. Strange, all the permutations flesh can take, all the ways the body heals itself, even when attempts have been made to destroy it. And yet it's so normal, so less dramatic than what I'd imagined. The scars are difficult to see, not because they're offensive, but because each one is evidence of something withstood or inflicted. You're so damaged. How could I have not known this? How could I not have seen this?

> WILLEM *puts his hands under* JUDE*'s T-shirt.* JUDE *wakes up and startles, crawling to another place like a feral animal.*

It'll be a good thing for you. I promise you, Jude.

> JUDE *undresses under the blankets.* WILLEM *carefully places his hand on* JUDE*'s back.*

And I put my hand on your neck…I put my hand here, on your shoulders…I put my hand on your upper arms…I put my hand on your lower back…between your shoulder blades…

> JUDE *begins to cry furiously. He cries like he hasn't cried in a long time.*

I'm afraid; for the first time, I'm really afraid. I knew you were inhibited. Extremely inhibited. But now I know it's not a reluctance to have sex, it's a terror of it. But what do I do? It's been a long time since I've wanted anyone so badly.

JUDE. I'm sorry.

WILLEM. No, I'm sorry.

JUDE. Willem, if you want to reconsider, I understand.

WILLEM. Of course I don't want to.

JUDE. Come here.

WILLEM. Jude…

JUDE. I'm going to try again.

WILLEM. Are you sure?

JUDE. Yes.

They make love.

WILLEM. Was it okay?

JUDE. Yes, Willem, it was okay. (*To himself.*) It'll be better next time.

ANA. And if it's not?

JUDE. Then maybe the time after that.

WILLEM. Did you really like it, Jude?

JUDE. Am I not doing a good enough job?

WILLEM. What? No. I mean, yes. What do you mean?

JUDE *kisses* WILLEM. *It is the first time in his life that he has initiated a kiss.*

JUDE. It'll be all right, Willem.

WILLEM. Yes.

JUDE. I'll always take care of you, you know that, don't you?

WILLEM. I know. I do know. (*Pause.*) Jude, how would you feel about us building a house together?

JUDE. Our house...

WILLEM. I've seen a piece of land, just an hour north of the city. There's a lake, and a forest as well. We could build something there—it'd be ours.

JUDE (*to himself*). A house—a house in a forest.

WILLEM. Jude? What's wrong?

JUDE. Nothing. Nothing. Yes, Willem—I think we should do it.

WILLEM. And I have something else to ask you.

Jude. Is there a reason you can't have erections?

JUDE. It's because of—because of the car injury.

ANA. A lie.

WILLEM. Is there nothing that could help? Could you try something—a shot, a pill?

JUDE. No. I can't. I'm allergic to those medications.

ANA. A lie.

WILLEM. Should we try something different?

JUDE. Willem, you have to stop asking me. You're making me feel like a freak.

WILLEM. I'm sorry, Jude. I didn't mean to. I just want you to enjoy this.

JUDE. I am.

What if it never stops? What if I'm never allowed to stop? What am I going to do then?

3.

JUDE. Rule number one: Never refuse Willem. He's sacrificed so much for me. Two: Remember what Brother Luke taught me, and show a little enthusiasm.

BROTHER LUKE. Roll over. Make some noise. Say you like it.

JUDE. Three: Initiate sex once every three times.

BROTHER LUKE. Your competency will conceal your lack of enthusiasm.

JUDE. Four: Whatever Willem wants me to do, I'll do.

ANA. Five: Trust Willem.

JUDE. But I trusted Brother Luke, too…

ANA. Don't compare him to Willem.

JUDE. But they both want the same thing. When it's over, there's the same shame. What's the difference?

ANA. To be able to give pleasure to the person you care about most.

JUDE. Not having sex: it's one of the best things about being an adult.

It's night. JUDE *gets up to sneak into the bathroom. Suddenly he feels* WILLEM*'s hand.*

WILLEM. Where're you going?

JUDE. Let me go.

They look at each other for a long time.

Let me go, Willem, I'm serious.

WILLEM. No, Jude. I can't have you doing this to yourself.

JUDE. I need to go to the bathroom.

WILLEM. All right, let's go then. I'm going to watch you.

JUDE. Stop it, Willem—stop it. You're treating me like a child.

WILLEM. Don't you understand why this upsets me?

JUDE. You have to trust me.

WILLEM. I *do* trust you. That isn't the issue. The issue is you hurting yourself.

JUDE. You have to let me do it, Willem. I'm insufferable if I don't.

WILLEM. Who would you be without it?

JUDE. Let it go, Willem, please.

WILLEM. Try, Judy. Try for me. Promise?

JUDE. I—I promise.

ANA. Count your breaths.

JUDE. It doesn't work. I've been counting a whole hour now. I imagine myself in one of the motel rooms, throwing myself against a wall. But all I can think about is the razor.

I can't expect you to understand what it does for me, how it makes me feel that my body and my life are mine, and mine alone. I can't expect you to understand that there's no way we're having sex if I don't cut myself.

JUDE *goes to the bathroom. The extensive scarring on his forearms force him to cut his triceps instead, and he regrets not being able to see the cuts as he makes them. Suddenly, he looks up and sees* WILLEM *standing in front of him.* JUDE *shrinks against the sink and* WILLEM *squats down and takes the razor from his hand. They look at it for a moment. Then* WILLEM *stands and pulls the blade over his own chest.*

Willem, no!

WILLEM. Fuck! *Fuck!*

A second cut.

JUDE. Stop it, Willem. Stop it! You're hurting yourself.

WILLEM. You see what it feels like? You see what it feels like, Jude?

A third cut.

JUDE. Please stop, Willem, please, please.

And another. And another. And another. Six cuts in total.

WILLEM. Jesus Christ, this hurts.

JUDE. But you need to bandage them.

WILLEM. Bandage your own goddamned arms. This isn't some fucked-up ritual we're going to share, bandaging each other's cuts.

JUDE. I'm sorry.

Silence. They calm down.

WILLEM. Jesus, Jude, this really hurts. How can you stand this?

JUDE. You get used to it.

WILLEM (*crying*). Jude—are you even happy with me?

JUDE. Willem. You've made me happier than I've ever been in my life.

MALCOLM. Guys, I went up to see the property—it's a beautiful piece of land. Thirty acres, with its own lake and its own forest. I'll have a path created through the forest so you can walk around the lake. We'll have herbs planted between each of the flagstones, so when you step on them, you'll smell their perfume. There's a meadow, and a barn just beyond it. And as for the house—I thought: Something glass, with big rooms. During the day, you won't need to use lamps; at night, it'll glow like a lantern. You're going to love it there. I drew some plans that we should look at.

WILLEM. Mal, I trust you.

JUDE. But I'll look at them with you.

MALCOLM. Of course you will!

JUDE. A house in a forest.

MALCOLM. *Your* house, Jude. Yours and Willem's.

JUDE. I don't know how to thank you, Mal. But isn't a project like this boring for you?

MALCOLM. No. It's true that a building is an expression of form, but it's also a shelter—it's someplace you'll feel safe, where nothing will be able to touch you or find you, someplace that belongs to you and only you.

What better job is there than to create a place like that for two people I love so much? What's more important than that?

4.

ANA. Willem leaves to shoot a film, and the hyenas return.

JUDE. After we began having sex, they multiplied. They circle me, they lie splayed on the savanna, they stare at me with their yellow eyes.

ANA. They howl and howl.

JUDE. Yet I can't cut myself: I promised Willem.

JUDE *dips a paper towel in oil and rubs it on his arm. He takes a deep breath, lights the match and holds the flame to his arm until his skin catches fire.*

This scent—this scent of smoking olive oil—leads me to a night in Perugia where I had funghi with Willem, and then a Tintoretto exhibit I saw with Malcolm at the Frick, a boy in college I once knew named Frick, and then suddenly I'm in the monastery, and then the car, the car with Brother Luke, the time he stopped by the side of the road and we had sex in a field where they were harvesting hay, and the smell of the hay from the fields as it burned, and then, and then, and then…

He smells burnt meat and snaps out of his trance. When he realizes that it's his own arm, his own flesh he's smelling, he screams in horror and pain, turning on the faucet.

And now salt.

Sobbing, he rubs a handful of crystals into the burn, causing the pain to flare brighter.

Is this enough? Is this enough? Are you happy now?

ANDY. Jesus. What the fuck have you done?!

JUDE. I was frying plantains.

ANDY. You're lying.

JUDE. What do you mean?

ANDY. Jude—*what the fuck* have you done?!

JUDE. *I told you.*

ANDY. No. No. Jude, you're lying to me. You tell me what you've done right now. You…you…You're sick, Jude. You're crazy. This is behavior that could and should get you locked away for years. You're sick and you're crazy and you need help.

JUDE. Don't you *dare* call me crazy.

ANDY. You have to tell Willem this week. After that, I'm telling him myself.

JUDE. Andy, please. Please don't tell him. If you tell him, he'll leave me.

ANDY. Not this time. I'm not covering for you this time, Jude.

This is really going to hurt.

If you ruin this—if you keep lying to someone who loves you, who *really* loves you, who only wants to see you exactly as you are—it *will* be your fault. And it'll be your fault not because of what's been done to you or the diseases you have or what you think you look like, but because of *you*: Because you don't trust Willem, because you lie to him, because you won't treat him with the generosity he's *always* given you.

JUDE. No. No. I'm doing it to spare him. I'm doing it to protect him.

ANDY. You think you're sparing him, but you're not. You're selfish and proud and you're going to ruin the best thing that's happened to you.

JUDE. What do you want me to do, Andy?

ANDY. One week. You have one week, Jude.

WILLEM *comes home*.

JUDE. Willem…you're home. You don't know how much I missed you.

WILLEM. What is it? Jude?

JUDE. You know I'm trying not to cut myself.

WILLEM. I know.

JUDE. And I'm going to keep trying.

WILLEM. Yes.

JUDE. But sometimes I might not be able to control myself.

They are silent.

WILLEM. Jude, what's this on your arm? What happened? What did you do?

JUDE *mumbles something unintelligible.*

Louder. I can't hear you.

JUDE. I burned myself.

WILLEM (*furious*). How?

JUDE (*faintly*). There was olive oil—a fire.

WILLEM. You *set yourself on fire*? *Why*, Jude? Why did you do this!?

JUDE. I was trying not to cut myself.

They are silent.

That night. WILLEM *wakes up.* JUDE *isn't next to him in bed.*

WILLEM. Where is it?

JUDE. I'm not doing anything.

WILLEM. You're lying.

JUDE. I'm not—I'm not doing anything.

WILLEM *climbs on top of* JUDE. *He presses his knees into* JUDE*'s shoulders and tears at* JUDE*'s clothing, trying to rip them off. They struggle.*

WILLEM. Where is it?

JUDE. Please, Willem. Please. Please. Stop, Willem—please, stop. You're hurting me.

WILLEM. Where is it? Where's the fucking razor?

JUDE. Willem…

WILLEM. Here it is—I knew it. *I knew it.*

JUDE. Fine. You have it. Now get the fuck away from me and leave me alone.

WILLEM. You're sick. There's something seriously wrong with you. You need to be hospitalized. You need—

JUDE. Stop it, Willem, stop it. I don't need you to save me.

WILLEM. Oh, right, sorry—I forgot that you like to be kicked around in your relationships.

JUDE. Fuck off, Willem—what am I to you, anyway? I'm not your *goddamned* charity project.

WILLEM. Fine. Fine. Cut yourself to shreds. You love the cutting more than me, anyway.

WILLEM flings himself down on the couch, screaming into the pillow and kicking his arms and legs. Eventually JUDE creeps in, curling himself up in a corner of the room. WILLEM stands and leaves the room. He goes for a run to try to burn off some of the anger, which rises and fades in him by the step.

ANA. Make him talk to you.

When WILLEM returns, JUDE is still in the same spot. WILLEM lies down next to him, puts his arms around him.

WILLEM. I'm sorry, Jude, I'm sorry. I never, ever should have gotten so physical with you.

JUDE. I'm sorry, too. I'm sorry about what I said. I'm sorry I lied to you.

WILLEM. You know, Jude—being with you is sometimes like walking through this fantastic landscape. You think it's a forest, and then suddenly it changes into a meadow, or cliffs of ice. And they're all beautiful, but they're strange as well.

And you don't have a map, so you try to adjust as you go, but you don't know what you're doing, and so sometimes you make mistakes. Bad mistakes. That's what it feels like.

JUDE. So basically, you're saying I'm New Zealand.

WILLEM. Yes. Yes, you're New Zealand.

JUDE. Are you going to leave?

WILLEM. No. I don't think so. But I do think you need help. Help I don't know how to give you. (*Pause.*) I either want you to start seeing a psychologist—or I want you to voluntarily commit yourself to a hospital.

JUDE. And what if I don't want to do either? Are you going to leave?

WILLEM. Jude. I can't stay to watch you do this to yourself—not if you'd interpret my presence as tacit approval. So. I guess I would.

JUDE. If I tell you—if I tell you everything I can't discuss—do I still have to go get help?

WILLEM. Oh, Jude. Yes, you still have to. But I hope you'll tell me anyway. Whatever it is; whatever it is.

ANA. And then, at last, Jude starts talking. On and on he speaks, and Willem listens. It's often difficult for him to speak, and the two of them are often silent. Sometimes their silence turns to sleep. And then Willem hears Jude's voice again, and he wakes and he listens.

JUDE. Brother Luke was my father first, then he was my—

He promised me we would live in a cabin in the woods, or in a house by the sea. When I turned sixteen, we'd get married and go on a honeymoon. He would buy me a piano so I could play and sing. When I turned sixteen, I could stop. But I had so long to wait.

BROTHER LUKE. You've grown so much, Jude. You'll be a teenager before you know it.

JUDE. Sometimes, after a group would visit, I couldn't work for days—it was too painful. But Brother Luke would try to cheer me up.

BROTHER LUKE. You liked that last one, am I right, Jude? There's nothing to be ashamed of—I heard you enjoying yourself. That's good. It's good to enjoy your work. But you have to stop throwing yourself against the wall. The clients don't like seeing you all bruised.

JUDE (*to* BROTHER LUKE). It hurts.

BROTHER LUKE. I'm sorry, Jude, I'm sorry—but you have to keep going.

JUDE. I want to stop. Please, let me stop.

BROTHER LUKE. Soon, soon, Jude.

JUDE. When?

BROTHER LUKE. When you're sixteen.

JUDE. But that's so far away!

BROTHER LUKE. Then we'll get married. Not father and son, but a married couple. We'll go on a honeymoon. Isn't it wonderful to look forward to that?

ANA. Sometimes you're unable to continue, and Willem holds you so tightly that you can't breathe. Sometimes you try to break free; Willem pins you down until you give up.

BROTHER LUKE. You know, Jude, when people love each other as much as you and I do, they sleep in the same bed, and they kiss each other. I don't allow the clients to kiss you—only I can, because we're in love.

JUDE. I've tried to be another person. A better person. I tried to make myself clean. But I can't, I can't.

BROTHER LUKE. Come here, Jude, my sweetheart. We're going to have fun tonight. Just you and me. It's going to feel so different, you'll see—because we love each other; because we're in love.

He pulls JUDE *against himself.*

My baby: Wasn't that nice? Didn't it feel different?

JUDE. Nobody has ever been as good to me as Brother Luke. He fed me, he taught me. He never hit me, not once. When I was with the clients, he was always on the other side of the wall, listening, making sure they didn't hit me, either.

WILLEM. He was a monster, Jude.

JUDE. I need to believe that, in spite of everything, Brother Luke really loved me.

WILLEM. He didn't, Jude. He just said that so he could manipulate you.

JUDE. He lied to me and did horrible things to me, but I need to believe that part was real.

WILLEM. That's what pedophiles do.

JUDE. When Caleb was raping me, I imagined that Brother Luke was hiding in the bathroom and would jump out to help me if things got too bad.

WILLEM. You were a child. He took advantage of you. Don't you see that? Can't you understand that?

JUDE. The truth is: In everything I do, in everything I am, there's Brother Luke. My love of reading, of music, of math, of languages, of gardening, of cooking. He gave me all of those things. All of those are his.

WILLEM *cries*.

WILLEM. When did it stop?

JUDE. One night—we'd just had sex; I was twelve—there was a banging on the door. *Edgar Wilmot, open up!*

BROTHER LUKE (*to* JUDE). Quiet. Don't make a sound.

ANA. Edgar Wilmot, this is the police! Open this door immediately!

BROTHER LUKE. It's going to be okay. Don't worry; don't worry.

ANA. Edgar Wilmot, we have a warrant for your arrest. Open this door!

BROTHER LUKE. I'll be right back. Stay here.

JUDE. The police break down the door, and Brother Luke runs into the bathroom.

No, Brother Luke! Don't leave me here! Don't leave me alone!

ANA. Jude St Francis?

JUDE. Yes.

ANA. Jude. It's okay. You're safe now.

JUDE. One of the police officers helps me dress. I need Brother Luke, I need him to protect me: *Brother Luke!*

ANA. Jude, what happened to you?

JUDE. I break free, run towards the bathroom.

ANA. No, don't!

JUDE. ...where Brother Luke is hanging from the ceiling, an extension cord around his neck.

ANA. How often have you been raped?

JUDE. What do you mean?

ANA. How often have you had sex?

JUDE. With Brother Luke, or with the others?

ANA. What others?

JUDE. There are so many. And as I tell her, the woman looks away. Then I know for certain that what I've done is wrong. I feel so ashamed, so dirty, that I want to die.

ANA. They are silent again, and they sleep. They don't know the time, only that a day has come and gone. Willem listens to stories that are unimaginable, abominable. At times he wants to cover Jude's mouth to make the stories stop.

WILLEM. And after that?

JUDE. After Brother Luke?

WILLEM. Yes.

JUDE. After that I was sent to the home. Everyone knew who I was and what I had done. The counselors there did what so many men had done to me all along. One night I made a run for it, away from the home, away from it all. It felt like ecstasy, running down those empty streets. I ran and ran until I couldn't any longer, and then I fell asleep behind a gas station. When I woke, I was in the back seat of a car, and there was Schubert playing. I was comforted by that, and I fell asleep again. And when I woke next, I was in a living room.

TRAYLOR. Come to the kitchen—I'll give you something to eat.

JUDE. Thank you.

TRAYLOR. You're a prostitute, right?

JUDE. Yes.

TRAYLOR. For how long?

JUDE (*silence*).

TRAYLOR. Two years? Five years? Ten? Your whole life?

JUDE. Five years.

> The man is annoyed, but his voice is soft.

TRAYLOR. You have a venereal disease. I can smell it on you. But you're in luck—I'm a doctor. I'll give you some antibiotics.

JUDE. He walks to a door, unlocks it, and opens it.

> He remains silent. I prepare myself for the man to be cruel; the quiet ones always are.

TRAYLOR. Day one.

JUDE. I'm expecting a dungeon, but it's a windowless basement bedroom, with cement floors and a blue blanket on the bed.

TRAYLOR. I put out some clothes for you.

JUDE. I know what to do, so as the man stares at me, I begin to unbutton my shirt. But he stops me.

TRAYLOR. You're sick. You have to get better first. The antibiotics take ten days to eliminate the infection. Don't tell me this is the first venereal disease you've ever had.

JUDE. Then he leaves the room. Every day it's the same pattern.

TRAYLOR. Day two.

JUDE. Eat. Rest. Medication. Silence doesn't make me nervous, but this man's silence is like a cat watching so fixedly that you don't know what it sees…

TRAYLOR. Day three.

JUDE. ...and then suddenly it will jump, and trap something beneath its paw.

TRAYLOR. Day four.

Day five.

Do you like being a prostitute?

JUDE. No.

TRAYLOR. Then why do you do it?

JUDE. It's what I know how to do.

TRAYLOR. Are you good at it?

JUDE. Yes.

TRAYLOR. No. You need to rest.

Day six.

Day seven.

JUDE. Wait. What's your name? My name's Joey.

TRAYLOR. Dr Traylor.

JUDE. I want to help with something. I can help you clean — or cook — or —

TRAYLOR. You're sick.

JUDE. I'm better.

TRAYLOR. No, you're sick, you have an infectious disease. I don't want you touching my food.

So. You don't want me to call you a prostitute?

JUDE. No.

TRAYLOR. But that *is* what you are, isn't it? Shall I call you a whore, maybe? Is that better?

JUDE. No.

TRAYLOR. So, prostitute it is, then, right?

JUDE. Yes.

TRAYLOR. Good.

JUDE. And then he leaves and I look for something to cut myself with, but there's nothing sharp in the room. So I press my nails into my calves, and finally I puncture the skin, and I work my nail back and forth in the cut to make it wider. I know that there is something wrong with Dr Traylor. *Help me, Brother Luke, help me.*

TRAYLOR. Day eight.

Day nine.

Day ten.

JUDE. On the eleventh day, the door opens, and he is standing there.

TRAYLOR *holds an iron fire poker in his hand.*

TRAYLOR. Take off your clothes.

JUDE *obeys.*

Take my pants down.

You try *anything*—biting, anything—and I'll beat you in the head with this until you're a vegetable, do you understand me?

JUDE (*silence*).

TRAYLOR. Speak!

JUDE. Yes, I understand.

Dr Traylor scares me. But Brother Luke has trained me too well: I'm a good prostitute. I don't fight back.

TRAYLOR. You had ten days of hospitality. It's time to repay those ten days.

JUDE. And then can I go?

TRAYLOR. See you tomorrow.

Day one.

Day two.

Day three.

JUDE. The sex is no worse than what I've had before, but I know that it's just prelude, that it will eventually get very bad.

TRAYLOR. Day four.

ANA. What comes next confirms everything you were afraid of.

TRAYLOR. Day five.

Day six.

JUDE. On the sixth day of the repayment I try to escape.

ANA. The punishment is terrible. The doctor unbuckles his belt and begins whipping you with it. Lash after lash, on your back, your legs, your neck. All you can hear is Dr Traylor's breaths, his gasps. All of your energy deserts you, like a flock of birds rising and swiftly flying away.

The sex also gets worse. You're made to do things that you'll never be able to talk about, not to anyone, not even to yourself. When you wake at night, you pray that you may die soon.

JUDE. Help me, Brother Luke. Help me. Protect me.

ANA. One day, after three or four months, Dr Traylor says:

TRAYLOR. I'm tired of you. You're dirty and you disgust me and I want you to leave.

JUDE. Okay. I'll leave now.

TRAYLOR. You'll leave how I want you to.

ANA. And you get locked up again. For several days, nothing happens. Your food is served to you on a newspaper. One day you look at the date...

JUDE. It's my birthday. I am fifteen.

ANA. That night, Dr Traylor comes downstairs with his fire poker.

TRAYLOR. Get up.

ANA. You stand up, tripping through the door, stumbling through the house. You're prodded to the front door, and then outside, into the night. Even through your fear and the cold you notice something.

JUDE. I can smell the air turning green. It's spring.

TRAYLOR. Get in the car!

ANA. Dr Traylor opens the trunk.

JUDE. I can't.

ANA. You're so weak that the doctor has to help you. The car starts. It drives over some uneven surface and stops.

For three minutes nothing happens.

JUDE. I hear nothing except my own breath, my own heart.

ANA. Then the trunk opens. Dr Traylor shoves you to the front of the car with the fire poker.

TRAYLOR. Stay there.

ANA. You obey.

TRAYLOR. And now run.

ANA. You stand still.

TRAYLOR. You like running so much, right? So run.

ANA. Dr Traylor starts the engine.

Wake up, Jude. You have to start running.

TRAYLOR. Start running, Joey.

Run faster!

Get up. Get up. Get up.

JUDE. I feel the headlights coming toward me, two streams of fire, and I turn my head to the side and wait, and the car comes toward me and drives over my legs. The angel wraps his wings around me. I turn to cinders and am gone, released from this world.

ANA. It is done.

Willem asks him again, and Jude takes a long time to answer. But it is an honest answer.

WILLEM. Have you *ever* enjoyed having sex? Even a little, even occasionally, at all?

JUDE. I always thought that someday, things would get better. As if age would transform sex into something glorious and enjoyable. But nothing has changed. Nothing.

WILLEM. I feel like I'm just another one of those men.

JUDE. Of course not. Of course you're not.

WILLEM. But I've made you do things you don't want to do.

JUDE. We can do whatever you want, Willem.

WILLEM. But you don't enjoy it.

JUDE. So what are we going to do?

WILLEM. I don't know. But we'll figure it out. I promise we will.

JUDE. Together?

WILLEM. Yes. Together.

Part VII

1.

Lantern House, Garrison.

MALCOLM. Here it is—Lantern House.

JUDE. I love it here, Malcolm. I don't know how to thank you.

MALCOLM. I keep telling you—you don't have to thank me. You saw I cut this path around the lake, right?

JUDE (*teasingly*). Yes—and I also saw that you placed benches along the path.

MALCOLM. Not because I think you *can't* walk it, Judy—it's just in case.

JUDE. I know, I know. You're right, Malcolm. You were always right. You always knew what I needed, even when I couldn't admit it to myself.

MALCOLM. Well, that's not my place, is it?

JUDE. What, to make me face reality?

MALCOLM. No. Not my way.

JUDE. I know. And I'm so lucky for that, Mal.

MALCOLM. But Jude—you have to stop seeing these benches as reminders of what you *can't* do. Couldn't you try seeing them as something else instead?

Like how I saw them: You and Willem walking through the forest, and around the lake. You stop at the second bench, see, and it offers a direct view of the house across the water. You sit down, together; you look at the house you live in, together; you stand back up, together; you keep walking, together.

JUDE. Mal—you were always more poetic than I am.

MALCOLM. That's not true. You just don't have enough imagination when it comes to your own life.

2.

WILLEM (*to* JUDE). Well...do you think he's wrong?

JUDE. You clearly don't think he is!

WILLEM. You have a lot of imagination about other people's lives. But it's true—you do have difficulty thinking of yourself differently.

It's why I sometimes think I care more about you being alive than you do.

JUDE. No, Willem. You can't say that. I mean...maybe, at one point. But not any longer.

WILLEM. Come here. Dance with me.

JUDE. You know I can't dance.

WILLEM. Just one. I'll help you.

Put your arms around me. Put your right foot back as I put my left foot forward.

They dance.

See? You're dancing.

JUDE. I'm not very good at it.

WILLEM. You're perfect at it.

JUDE. I'm afraid I'm going to fall.

WILLEM. I'll hold you.

As they dance, it's clear JUDE*'s in greater and greater pain. He continues to move, but barely. Eventually they just rock back and forth without their feet lifting off the ground. When the song ends, cheers go up.*

3.

ANDY. Jude, only you know how much pain you can tolerate. But there are some realities to consider here. Every time I see you, you've gotten a little weaker. The treatments aren't working. The wounds aren't healing. And you've lost way too much weight.

If you do this, I promise you that your quality of life will improve instantly. The prosthetics available now are so infinitely superior that your gait will be more natural than it is with your actual legs. I'll do the surgery myself, and you'll be home in less than a week.

JUDE. And what happens if I say no?

ANDY. If you say no, we keep pushing forward on everything we've been trying and hope something eventually works.

JUDE. I won't let Dr Traylor determine the shape of my life. I can't. I can't let him win.

ANDY (*to* WILLEM). I promise you I'll take care of him.

WILLEM. I know.

ANDY. Jude, count backwards from ten for me.

JUDE. Ten, nine, eight, seven...

WILLEM. You can't die, Jude. You can't. All these years, and I haven't really prepared myself. I don't know what it means if you're no longer here. If you get better, I promise you more patience, more gratitude. I promise you less vanity, less selfishness, less complaining, less fear.

I promise you. You just have to survive.

4.

JUDE. Where am I? Who am I?

ANDY. You're Jude St Francis.

WILLEM. You're my oldest, dearest friend.

HAROLD. You're the son of Harold Stein.

MALCOLM. The friend of Malcolm Irvine.

JB. Of Jean-Baptiste Marion.

ANDY. Of Andy Contractor.

MALCOLM. You're a New Yorker. You live in SoHo. You're a lawyer. You volunteer for an arts non-profit and a soup kitchen.

HAROLD. You're a swimmer. You're a baker. You're a cook. You're a reader.

WILLEM. You have a beautiful voice, though you never sing anymore.

JB. You're an art collector.

WILLEM. You write me lovely messages. You're patient. You're generous. You're the best listener I know.

MALCOLM. The smartest person I know.

ANDY. The bravest person I know.

JB. You love your job.

HAROLD. You're a mathematician. You're a logician.

All except WILLEM *disappear.*

WILLEM. You were treated horribly. You came out the other end. You were always you.

JUDE. And who are you?

WILLEM. I'm Willem Ragnarsson. And I will never let you go.

5.

Three months later. JUDE *and* WILLEM *are in the kitchen at Lantern House. They've just cooked together.*

JUDE. When I was fifteen and couldn't trust people, Ana said to me that if I let it, the rest of my life would be blessed, that I would meet only good people. I didn't believe her. I wanted to—but I couldn't.

But look—she was right after all. People kept entering my life, bequeathing me with generosities. People so different from the ones I once knew that they seemed to be another species altogether. It's as if life wasn't just making up for those first fifteen years, but was begging my forgiveness, piling riches on me, smothering me in all the things I hoped for.

There was only one condition: I had to trust. I had to hope. And if I did, I would be lucky for my entire life.

(*To* WILLEM.) Aren't you picking up Malcolm and JB from the train station?

WILLEM. Shit, you're right.

WILLEM leaves. At the station only MALCOLM is waiting.

MALCOLM. JB didn't come.

WILLEM. Why not?

MALCOLM. He and his boyfriend broke up — maybe — this morning.

WILLEM. And how about you? How's life as a married man?

MALCOLM *laughs*.

It's a thirty-minute drive back to the house. But even though I'm not hurrying, I don't see the truck coming at us in the intersection until it's too late. By the time I feel the crunch, I'm already being ejected into the air. 'No!' I shout. 'Malcolm!' And then I see a flash of Jude's face.

But my final thoughts are not of Jude, but of my brother, Hemming. Hemming was eight when I was born. He couldn't walk or speak, but I never thought of him as anything other than my older brother. *I* thought we looked like brothers, but no one else seemed to notice. They saw only that he was in a wheelchair, with his mouth open.

When he was hospitalized for the final time, I was in college. And when he died, I realized, in a way I never had before, that I had lost something essential in my life. And now I see him again: He's sitting in his wheelchair on the lawn in front of our home, staring at me with the kind of steady gaze he was never able to give me in life. *Hemming*, I shout, *wait for me!* And I run to my brother, faster and faster — so fast that I can no longer feel the ground beneath me.

Part VIII

1.

HAROLD *calls. Answering machine.*

HAROLD. Jude. Next week is Thanksgiving. I need to see you. Anywhere. With whomever you want. Or no one.

HAROLD *calls. Answering machine.*

It'll get better. I swear. It won't seem like it now, but it will. I know. I promise you.

JB *calls. Answering machine.*

JB. Hey Judy, it's me. I'm just checking in on you. I've been thinking about you a lot. I'd like to see you. Love you. Bye.

JB *calls. Answering machine.*

Hey Judy. I was thinking about the four of us. And now it's just you and me. At least we have each other.

2.

JUDE *is extremely emaciated. He has noticed that if he does not eat for long enough, he can go to the limit of unconsciousness, so that he hallucinates and* WILLEM *appears.*

JUDE (*singing*).
> *Ich bin der Welt abhanden gekommen,*
> *Mit der ich sonst viel Zeit verdorben.*

ANDY. Get up, Jude. Get up. You can't, can you? You've lost so much weight that your prostheses no longer fit, am I right? When I last saw you, you were already down ten pounds. How much is it now? Twenty? More? What're you doing to yourself?

JUDE *doesn't respond.*

You look terrible. You look sick.

JUDE *doesn't respond.*

Why are you doing this to yourself? Say something. Goddamn it, Jude.

A loss of one to ten percent of your body weight is Grade One. If you lose any more weight, we'll have to put you on a feeding tube, and you don't want that.

HAROLD. All you have got to do right now is eat. You're going to eat this now.

HAROLD *brings* JUDE *toast. Twice.* JUDE *refuses both times.* HAROLD *sits down with him and sings. It is a song* JUDE *has never heard before but which he instinctively recognizes as a lullaby.*

Jude. My poor Jude. My poor sweetheart.

My sweetheart. My darling. My baby.

3.

HAROLD. How do you keep someone alive who doesn't want to stay alive? First you try logic:

(*To* JUDE.) You have so much to live for.

Then you try guilt:

(*To* JUDE.) You owe me.

Then you try anger, and threats, and pleading:

(*To* JUDE.) I'm old; don't do this to an old man.

You have to tell yourself every day: *I am doing the right thing*. To let him do what he wants to do is abhorrent to the laws of love. But if your child is inconsolable, is it then your job to give him permission to leave?

I sometimes see him looking at something I can't see. Then he twitches his head, like a horse, and comes back to himself.

(*To* JUDE.) I think we should work on a project together. Maybe you can finally teach me how to cook. Otherwise, you'll be cooking for me when I'm a hundred.

(*To us*.) If he kills himself, I'll survive, but I know that surviving will be an ordeal. That is his power. He has that power, and I do not.

When you have a child, you find yourself feeling more assured with each month that passes and your child remains alive. You feel he's staking a claim to life itself: the longer he's in this world, the more deeply rooted he becomes. And yet this belief can be proven wrong in an instant, and my child has proven me wrong in the most horrible way.

And yet, still, you keep hoping: that life tethers life. But his life is like a hot-air balloon, staked to the earth with a long, twisted rope. And while he pulls and pulls at the rope in order to tug himself loose, to drift into the skies, down below, there is a knot of us trying to pull the balloon back to the ground. Frightened for him. Frightened of him.

4.

ANA. June twelfth. A day with no significant events. A nothing day. He is fifty-three, for not even three months. He injects an artery with air, and gives himself a stroke. He has to stick himself at least twice, with a needle whose gauge was as thick as a hummingbird's beak. An agonizing death.

You all died so young. Willem, Malcolm, Jude. Andy dies three years later of a heart attack.

HAROLD. And now it's just JB and me. JB is sixty-one, I am eighty-four.

JB. I make one last series of my friends. Well, of Jude. Fifteen paintings of him, depicting imagined moments of his life from the years after Willem died.

HAROLD. I cannot look at them.

ANA. What else? Harold finally opens the letter that Jude left for him.

HAROLD. Eight pages. About Brother Luke and Dr Traylor, about what had happened to him. I kept putting the pages down and walking away from them, trying to find the courage to read some more. It took me days to finish it. 'I'm sorry,' he wrote. 'Please forgive me.' That he died still stubbornly believing everything Brother Luke, Dr Traylor, and the home said he was to be true; that he died thinking that even after all of us who loved him, makes me think that my life has been a failure after all.

I find myself wishing I believed in some sort of life after life, where he is that grey cat that has begun to sit outside our house, purring when I reach my hand out to it. Or maybe he is that flower that suddenly blooms on the rhododendron bush I thought had died long ago. Maybe he is that cloud, that mist, that rain. It isn't only that he died, or how he died; it is what he died believing.

And so I try to be kind to everything I see. And in everything I see, I see him.

THE END

About the Authors

HANYA YANAGIHARA

Hanya Yanagihara is the author of three novels: *The People in the Trees* (2013), *A Little Life* (2015) and *To Paradise* (2022). She lives in New York.

KOEN TACHELET

Born in 1964 in Antwerp, Belgium, Koen Tachelet started his work in the theatre as international programmer at deSingel Arts Centre in Antwerp. He subsequently worked as communications officer for the Dutch theatre company Het Zuidelijk Toneel and scientific researcher at the University of Antwerp and the Flemish Theatre Institute. In 2001, he founded APT (Arts, Performance, Theatricality), a post-graduate training programme for performing artists—currently known under the name a.pass. Since 2001 he has been working as theatre scriptwriter and artistic collaborator for directors such as Ivo van Hove, Johan Simons, Jossi Wieler, Christoph Marthaler, Alain Platel, FC Bergman and many others. Between 2005 and 2010—together with Simons—he was the driving force behind the renewal of NTGent, the City Theatre in Gent, and joined Simons at the Münchner Kammerspiele, one of the leading theatres in Germany.

As a theatre scriptwriter, Tachelet has adapted novels, movie scripts and plays for the stage, including *The Asylum Seeker* (Arnon Grunberg), *Life is a Dream* (Calderón de la Barca), *Gen (What dare I think?)* (from *The Elementary Particles* by Michel Houellebecq), *Decalogue*, *Trois Couleurs: Bleu-Blanc-Rouge* (Kieslowski) and *Double Indemnity* (Cain/Wilder). With Johan Simons, he realised a trilogy based on the work of Joseph Roth

(*Hiob, Hotel Savoy, Radetzkymarsch*). For Ivo van Hove he adapted *The Fountainhead* (Ayn Rand) and two novels by Louis Couperus.

Koen Tachelet works in an international context, in particular for the Münchner Kammerspiele, the Ruhrtriënnale, the Wiener Burgtheater, International Theatre Amsterdam, and the opera houses of Paris, Salzburg and Amsterdam (*Fidelio*, *Entführung aus dem Serail*, Hertog Blauwbaard's *Burcht*). He collaborated with Ivo van Hove in Amsterdam (International Theatre Amsterdam), London (*All About Eve*) and Paris (*The Glass Menagerie* and *Le Tartuffe ou l'Hypocrite* at Théâtre de l'Odéon and La Comédie Française).

IVO VAN HOVE

Ivo van Hove is an award-winning director who has served as the General Director of the prestigious Internationaal Theater Amsterdam (formerly Toneelgroep Amsterdam) since 2001. His acclaimed productions continue to tour around the world and have earned him many international accolades, including a Tony Award, an Olivier Award, two Obie Awards, and multiple others in France, Belgium, and the Netherlands. van Hove is a Chevalier dans l'Ordre des Arts et des Lettres in France, a Commander of the Order of the Crown in Belgium, and the recipient of the 2019 Johannes Vermeer Award, the Dutch state prize of the arts.

Broadway and West End highlights include *West Side Story*; *The Human Voice* with Ruth Wilson; *Network* with Bryan Cranston; *The Crucible* with Saoirse Ronan, Ben Whishaw and Ciarán Hinds; *A View from the Bridge* with Mark Strong; *All About Eve* with Gillian Anderson and Lily James; and *Lazarus*, which he created with David Bowie and Enda Walsh.

Select international credits include the Dutch-language version of *A Little Life* (most recently at Edinburgh Festival Theatre and BAM in New York); Shakespeare's *Roman Tragedies* and *Kings of War*; Ingmar Bergman's *Scenes from a Marriage*; Ayn Rand's *The Fountainhead*; Henrik Ibsen's *Hedda Gabler* with Ruth Wilson; Luchino Visconti's *Obsession* with Jude Law; Anne Carson's version of *Antigone* with Juliette Binoche, and Tennessee Williams' *The Glass Menagerie* with Isabelle Huppert.

Opera directing highlights include *Don Giovanni* and *Dead Man Walking* for The Metropolitan Opera, New York; *Salome* for Dutch National Opera; *Boris Godunov* and *Don Giovanni* for Paris Opéra; the world premiere *Brokeback Mountain* for Teatro Real Madrid; *La clemenza di Tito* and *Idomeneo* in Brussels; *Der Ring des Nibelungen* at Opera Antwerpen; and *Mahagonny* in the Festival d'Aix-en-Provence.

www.nickhernbooks.co.uk

facebook.com/nickhernbooks

twitter.com/nickhernbooks